Tristan Reached The Pool's Edge At The Same Time The Woman In The Pink Bikini Pulled Herself Out Of It.

With her hair pouring like wheat-colored silk down her back, her glistening body might have belonged to a swimsuit model—buxom with shapely tanned legs that just kept getting longer.

Tristan braced his own legs shoulder width apart and crossed his arms in a confrontational pose. Unsuspecting, the woman straightened fully, sliding her hands back over her hair, like some Bond Girl from a beach scene. When she finally noticed him—when she looked up with those big blue, suddenly startled eyes...

Tristan's mouth fell open and his arms dropped like dead weights to his sides. Then he dragged a hand down over his mouth and blinked several incomprehensible times.

No, this didn't make sense. The hair was the wrong color. That body sure as hell didn't fit. Still, he ground out the question.

"Ella...is that you?"

Dear Reader,

My all-time favorite fairy tale is Cinderella. When my sister gave me the picture book many years ago, I pored over the words, copied the illustrations, dreamed about being part of such a perfect ever-after.

The theme of rags to riches—from poor in life to rich in love—is still a favorite. Surely the ultimate fantasy is overcoming great odds to end up with a "prince" and lasting love.

My heroine in this story has faced many challenges. Illness and death in the family, accusations of murder, as well as chilling blackmail threats. Enough pressure for Ella Jacob to go underground and assume an identity as a dowdy but efficient housekeeper.

Her boss, successful businessman Tristan Barkley, is cynical about many things, but not where his housekeeper is concerned. Knowing Ella will make an ideal wife—certain that love will grow—he proposes marriage. But there's a price to pay for his readiness to trust so quickly, and a few more secrets to uncover about his new bride's past before they can come close to a fairy-tale ending.

Deceit, betrayal, deepest loyalty and even a touch of magic, I hope you enjoy *Bedded by Blackmail*.

Best,

Robyn

ROBYN GRADY

BEDDED BY BLACKMAIL

Silhouette®
Desire

Published by Silhouette Books
America's Publisher of Contemporary Romance

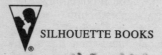

SILHOUETTE BOOKS

ISBN-13: 978-0-373-76950-6

Recycling programs
for this product may
not exist in your area.

BEDDED BY BLACKMAIL

Copyright © 2009 by Robyn Grady

Visit Silhouette Books at www.eHarlequin.com

Printed in U.S.A.

Books by Robyn Grady

Silhouette Desire

The Magnate's Marriage Demand #1842
For Blackmail...or Pleasure #1860
Baby Bequest #1908
Bedded by Blackmail #1950

ROBYN GRADY

left a fifteen-year career in television production knowing that the time was right to pursue her dream of writing romance. She adores cats, clever movies and spending time with her wonderful husband and their three precious daughters. Living on Australia's glorious Sunshine Coast, her perfect day includes a beach, a book and no laundry when she gets home.

Robyn loves to hear from readers. You can contact her at www.robyngrady.com.

For Carol, my beautiful big sister.
Happy birthday!

With thanks to my editor, Diana Ventimiglia,
for your help in making this book so special.

One

Tristan Barkley knew danger when he sensed it. As he whipped open the sliding glass door and scanned his expansive backyard, he sensed it in spades.

His heart beat like a war drum against his ribs while the hair on his nape prickled and every muscle in his body bunched tight.

Where was Ella? What trouble was she in?

He'd phoned to speak with his housekeeper twice this morning. Ella wasn't aware of his last-minute plans to attend a gala event in Sydney tonight. Home a day early from a weeklong trip to Melbourne, he'd wanted to be sure his tuxedo was back from the cleaners.

But when she hadn't answered his calls, he hadn't been concerned. Perhaps she was out shopping. Ella Jacob was fanatical about having her boss's every need and want satisfied. It was one of the reasons he valued her—or rather, her dedication to her job—so highly.

However, when he'd arrived home a few minutes ago, he'd noticed her car keys hanging on their hook. A second later, his gut wrenched at the sight of her practical leather handbag and its contents strewn over the kitchen counter. Her uniform had been turned inside out and discarded on the cold marble tiles. One black lace-up shoe lay near the timber meals table, the other had been left upside down near this door.

Now as he shaded his eyes against a single ray piercing the brewing black sky, his heart squeezed like a fist in his chest.

If anyone had entered his house uninvited…if someone had dared to hurt Ella…

He strode onto the lawn and movement beyond the northern courtyard caught his eye. Tristan narrowed his focus and zeroed in on a trespasser's fluid backstroke as the intruder sliced through the cool blue of his Olympic-size pool. Twenty-twenty vision said the long, tanned limbs were female. A flash of a pink swimsuit, and the curves it partially concealed, confirmed she was of his generation or younger.

Tristan let out a territorial growl. There'd been a recent spate of robberies in his neighborhood. The police suspected the work of a couple. One poor grandmother had been assaulted and tied up in her own home. Was that woman in his pool the girlfriend of some brazen burglar? he wondered.

He charged forward even as another scenario came to mind. Might be that Ella had simply invited a friend over. Although, come to think of it, he'd never heard her speak of friends. Or family. And that didn't explain the handbag, her uniform. It didn't explain where she was.

His long strides picked up pace.

Once he yanked that woman from the water, *hell 'n' Hades*, he'd have some answers then.

He reached the pool's edge at the same time the woman in pink climbed out, her hair falling like wheat-colored silk down her back. Her glistening body might have belonged to a swimsuit model—buxom with shapely, tanned legs that seemed to go on forever.

Tristan braced his own legs shoulder-width apart and crossed his arms. Unsuspecting, the woman straightened fully, sliding her hands back over her hair, like some Bond girl from a beach scene. When she finally noticed him, when she looked up with those big blue, suddenly startled eyes…

Tristan's mouth fell open and his arms dropped to his sides like dead weights. Then he dragged a hand down over his mouth and blinked several times.

No, this didn't make sense. The hair was the wrong color. That body sure as hell didn't fit. Still, he ground out the question.

"*Ella*…is that you?"

"Mr. Barkley?" The bombshell's cheeks turned as red as the miniature roses spilling from the poolside terracotta pots. "You weren't supposed to be back until tomorrow."

"I rang this morning." *Twice.*

Driven by testosterone-fueled force, his gaze dipped lower and his blood began to stir. Mother of mercy, he'd had no idea.

She folded her arms over the top of the swimsuit,

which only made her amazing cleavage appear twice as deep and ten times more alluring. This couldn't be the same woman…

"I rolled my ankle on a run this week," she explained. "I like to keep fit. Swimming's a good alternative." Her wet hair sprayed a cold arc on his business shirt as she threw a look at the pool then back. "I didn't think you'd mind."

His brain stumbled up to speed. Ella, his unassuming housekeeper, ran to keep fit? In a dowdy uniform, who'd have guessed she worried about anything other than making sure the bathroom sparkled and her delicious dinners were set on the table on time. Out of uniform, however, in that amazing swimsuit, she looked nothing short of…*sensational*.

As telltale heat flared through his system, he shook himself and squared his shoulders. That kind of reaction was totally inappropriate. Miss Jacob was the hired help—his housekeeper—and she still had more than a little explaining to do.

He cleared the thickness from his throat and stabbed a reproving finger toward the house. "Your uniform and shoes were tossed around the kitchen. Your handbag was tipped upside down on the counter."

What was he supposed to have thought? He'd been worried. Damn near frantic, in fact.

Her sheepish gaze dropped away. "Oh, that."

His brow furrowed more. "Yes. Dammit. *That*."

Dripping over the tiles, she began to move away. "It's kind of hard to explain."

"Like it's hard to explain how your hair's gone from mousy brown to blond?"

Had he landed in Wonderland? What was going on!

"I've only dyed it back to my natural color." She shrugged and explained, "I'm a woman. I wanted a change. This week I wanted to change it back."

He growled loud enough to be heard. She was avoiding his question. He wasn't a hard boss; he deserved her respect. The respect he'd always received from Ella in the past. Unless...

His thoughts froze as a withering feeling dropped through his center.

His voice deepened with concern. "Are you in some kind of trouble, Ella? Trouble you don't want to tell me about?"

When she blinked at him over her shoulder, her full lips slightly parted, she looked so vulnerable.

She curled strands of blond behind her ear. "I'm not in trouble. In fact, it's rather the opposite."

She continued on toward a sun lounger, her step favoring one leg. A very nice leg. Very nice body.

Tristan growled again.

He needed to get to the bottom of this mystery and he needed to do it now!

She picked up a towel from the sun lounger's back and wrapped it around herself, sari style. When she turned toward the house, he barred her way.

His voice was rough, his gaze unremitting. "I need an answer, Ella."

She peered up at him as rivulets of water trickled down her flawless face. Her eyes were the color of Ceylon sapphires. How had he missed that before? Did she usually wear glasses? He didn't think so.

Ella's mouth opened then shut. Finally she blew out a defeated breath. "I was going to tell you tomorrow."

He set his hands on his hips. His patience was wearing out. "I suggest you tell me now."

Her chin lifted slightly. "I'd like to hand in my resignation. I'm giving you two weeks' notice."

Tristan's usually balanced world tilted then slid off its axis. He ran a hand through his hair. Of all the crazy things, this had been the farthermost from his mind.

"You want to *leave*. Is it the pay?" Her wage was more than generous, but if that was the problem, it could easily be solved. "Name your price."

She was the best housekeeper he'd ever had—thorough, autonomous, inconspicuous, or at least she had been until this incident. He wasn't prepared to let her go, particularly not now.

The newly elected mayor of a neighboring smaller city had invited himself to dinner in three weeks' time. A positive impression could only help with an important deal Tristan had been working on, a project upon which he'd spent a vast amount of time and money. Obviously Ella's fine cooking skills wouldn't make or break the deal with Mayor Rufus. However, given the querulous past he and the mayor shared, frankly, Tristan could use all the help he could get.

A quiet strength shone from Ella's jeweled eyes. "Money's not the issue."

A recent memory popped into his head, and then he knew. Of course he knew.

Tristan scratched his temple and replaced the gravel in his voice with a more understanding tone. "Look, if this is about that episode before I left…"

The red in her cheeks spread down the column of her throat. Her chest rose and fell as she shook her head and, dodging him, moved away. "That morning has nothing to do with my leaving."

As his sense of control returned, Tristan eased out a relieved breath. Now that he knew what was behind her resignation, he could fix the situation.

He caught up, fell into step beside her and searched for words to handle this delicate matter.

"Admittedly it was an awkward moment," he said. "But there's no need to be embarrassed or do anything rash." His mind went back to that day. "You thought I'd already left for my week away in Melbourne," he recalled. "You didn't expect to see me in the bedroom, particularly without any clothes…"

His words trailed off as, head down, she limped faster.

That morning when he'd heard her gasp, he'd swung around and Ella's eyes had grown to the size of saucers. In that moment, he had reflexively stepped closer—to assure her not to be alarmed, nothing more. But he'd barely said her name before she'd scurried down the stairs like a frightened deer. After he'd dressed, he'd gone to smooth things over but had discovered that she'd left the house. With him away this week, they hadn't spoken of it…until now.

They lived together. Tricky situations were bound to occur, like her walking in on him buck-naked that morning, like his discovery of her swimming today—

He frowned.

Which brought him back to the original question.

"A resignation doesn't explain what happened to your

handbag." The way it had been upended as if some no-good scum had been in a hurry to get what he'd come for.

Her pace eased as she wrapped the towel more securely under her arms. "My inheritance from my mother finally came through." She flicked him a glance. "Nothing compared to your wealth, but enough that I shouldn't need to worry about money again if I'm careful. The executor organized to have the funds trans-ferred through to my account last night, but when it bounced back this morning, he rang to check the BSB number. After a few minutes, when I couldn't find the book I normally keep in my bag…" Her lips pressed together. "Well, I overreacted and dumped it upside down."

Tristan pictured the scene—Ella taking the call, the executor perhaps growing impatient when she'd kept him waiting. Her heart could have raced, her hands might have shaken. She was normally so composed and ordered, as was he. But having overreacted himself just now, he could better understand how she might have lost control in that moment.

"And the uniform? The shoes?"

Her face pinched, then she shrugged. "When I ended the phone call and knew the money would be in my account on Monday, I had this overwhelming urge to be free of them. I ripped the uniform off where I stood. Then I kicked off my shoes." She focused on her bare feet as she continued walking, moving slowly now. "I'm sorry. I didn't give any thought to where or how they landed."

Tristan slid his hands into his trouser pockets. So

Ella had come into an inheritance. Odd, but he'd never thought of her with parents. She'd seemed such a blank sheet. He hadn't known her business and she didn't ask about his. Not that there was much happening in his personal life these days.

He stood aside as she entered the kitchen through the still open door. "I'm sorry about your mother's passing," he offered.

Her step hesitated as she gave him a look he couldn't read. "She died eight months ago, just before I came to work for you."

As she moved into the kitchen, it struck him again that he knew nothing of his housekeeper's background. She'd shown up on his doorstep, explaining that she'd heard of the job opening. She hadn't presented references, which he usually would insist upon. But he'd taken her on, mainly because of a gut feeling that she would fit. Her reserved demeanor, her unassuming appearance, the way she'd quietly but succinctly responded to his questions—she'd simply felt…*right*.

As a rule he thought through every detail of a decision. He hated making a mistake. Growing up, his two brothers had called him Mastermind and had ribbed him constantly about his meticulous ways. Those days seemed so long ago. Although his younger brother hadn't visited this house in a long time, he and Josh kept in touch. However, he hadn't spoken to his older brother, Cade, in years. Never planned to again.

Ella made her way to the cushioned window seat and, wincing, sat.

He followed and indicated her ankle. "Mind if I have a look?" He'd been a lifeguard in his teens and early twenties and knew first aid. It could do more harm than good limping around when a joint needed rest.

She gave a reluctant nod and he dropped onto his haunches.

"The bruise is fading," she told him as he carefully turned the one-hundred-percent feminine ankle this way then that. "It wasn't so bad."

"Have you had it seen to?"

"No need. It's happened before, since as far back as junior high when I ran cross-country. I wear an ankle support and try not to overdo it, but I can't give up running. It's always been my release."

Well, this was the most information of a personal nature she'd ever offered. Was it because she was leaving? Because she was finally free and out of that drab past-the-knees dress that usually hid those honey-eyed shins. Shins that must feel as smooth as they looked.

When his fingertips tingled to inch higher, he bit down the urge, lowered her foot and pushed from his knees to stand.

Focus, Mastermind.

This was no time to slip up, even if Ella's transformation was one hellova jolt, as was her resignation. He'd gotten used to her living here. Where would she be bunking down two weeks from now?

"Have you arranged somewhere to live?" he asked.

Her blue eyes sparkled up at him. "I want to buy in an affordable neighborhood and rent something in the meantime."

Although he nodded sagely, it was almost painful to

think of not coming home to her. Despite checking her references, the housekeeper before Ella had been less than satisfactory—scorched shirts, mediocre meals. Ultimately, he'd had to let her go. Perhaps that's why he'd gone with gut rather than referecs in Ella's case.

And with Ella taking care of his domestic front, all had been as it should be. She knew exactly the right amount of ice to mix with his predinner Scotch. His sheets had never smelled better, of lavender and fresh sunshine. He trusted her, too, never needing to worry that some valuable item might go missing.

Damn.

He rubbed the back of his neck. "Two weeks, huh?"

Her smile was wry. "This is a luxurious setting with wonderful conditions. I doubt you'll have any trouble filling my spot."

"None who can cook like you."

Her head slanted at an amused angle as her eyes sparkled more. "Thank you. But my cooking's really nothing special."

Said who? He could practically smell her mouthwatering beef Wellington now. He particularly liked the way she distributed gravy—from a delicate, gold-rimmed pourer at the table, and only over the meat, never the vegetables. She always asked if there was anything else he'd like.

He'd always said no.

Tristan's stomach knotted and he cleared his throat. Hunger pains. He should've eaten on the plane.

He moved to his briefcase, which he'd left on the counter beside her upended handbag. "Whatever you do, however you do it, I've only ever received compliments from our dinner guests…and requests for invitations."

Most recently from Mayor Rufus.

As he clicked open his briefcase, out of the corner of his eye he saw Ella push to her feet. He could almost hear her thoughts.

"You've invited someone special to dinner, haven't you?"

He put on the eyeglasses he needed to read small print and shuffled through some property plans he ought to go over this afternoon. "I'll get around it."

Did he have any choice? Ella was obviously eager to start her new life, permanently shuck out of her "rags" and into something pretty. If no one else could make pork ribs with honey-whiskey sauce the way she did, he'd have to survive. He only wished the mayor, who had a notorious sweet tooth, hadn't heard Councilor Stevens's compliments regarding Ella's caramel apple pie.

Either way, the mayor had invited himself over, undoubtedly to kill two birds with one stone—sample Ella's superb culinary skills as well as address rezoning problems regarding acreage Tristan had purchased with a vast high-rise project in mind. But Tristan wasn't looking forward to another topic of conversation that would unfold during the course of the evening—conversation concerning a duplicitous and beautiful young woman who also happened to be the mayor's daughter…

Ella's voice came from behind him. "When did you invite them?"

"Really, Ella—"

"Tell me," she insisted.

He pushed out a sigh. "Three weeks. But it's fine."

"I could stay on a little longer, if that would help."

He slipped off his glasses, turned to her and smiled. Loyal to the end. "I wouldn't ask you to do that."

"Another week won't kill me." She flinched at her gaffe. "What I mean to say is, if one last dinner party will make a difference to an important business deal, I'll stay."

"I appreciate that, but as wonderful as your meals are, they're not a deal breaker."

She arched a knowing brow. "But it wouldn't hurt, right?"

Shutting his briefcase, he surrendered. "No. It wouldn't hurt."

"Then it's settled."

When she pulled back her shoulders, his jaw shifted. In the past, she'd never been the least assertive, but given she was only acting in his best interests he couldn't find a reason to object.

The real pity was he couldn't talk her into staying indefinitely. But why would—as it turned out—an attractive young lady remain as someone's housemaid when she had money enough to be independent? He had to be grateful she was willing to help out for an added week.

He swung his briefcase off the counter. "All right, I accept your offer. But I owe you."

Looking defensive, she moved to tidy her handbag mess. "You've already done enough."

"What? Allowed you to cook, clean and do my laundry?"

"You gave me a place to stay when I needed it most."

When she hesitated before dropping her purse into her handbag, Tristan studied her suddenly tight-lipped expression. Her background wasn't any of his business, particularly now that she'd resigned. Still, he was intrigued as he'd never been before. What harm would it do to get a little closer now that she was leaving? In fact, perhaps he could satisfy his curiosity over his unassuming duckling turned swan and at the same time thank Ella in some small but apt way.

He cocked his head. "I insist I repay the favor. What would you say to me supplying dinner for a change?"

Her eyes narrowed almost playfully as she stuffed the last article, a hairbrush, into her bag. "I didn't think you could cook."

"I can't. But I know a few chefs who can."

Her expression froze as a pulse beat high in her throat. She took a moment to speak. "You want to take me to dinner? But I'm your *housekeeper*."

"Only for another three weeks." But he didn't want to give her the wrong idea. "It's just a small show of appreciation for your efforts in the past, as well as for staying on longer than you'd intended."

It wasn't a date. Truth was he hadn't had a *real* date in a while. He didn't count the run of women he'd asked out once or twice to see if the chemistry worked.

He was thirty-two—time to find a wife and have that family. But with each passing birthday more and more he realized he preferred the old-fashioned type, and the women in his circle were either sickeningly simpering, over-opinionated or flat-out treacherous, as Bindy Rufus had been.

Ella crossed to the pot to make coffee—strong and fresh, just the way he liked it. Head bowed, she curled wet hair behind her ear and answered his question. "I don't think going out to dinner would be…appropriate."

"Then you need to think again." When he made up his mind, no one and nothing dissuaded him. Nevertheless, he put a smile into his voice. "Today's a day to kick off your shoes and let go, remember?"

She chewed her lower lip then, looking up at him, slowly grinned. "I guess it is."

Ignoring the embers that innocent smile stirred in the pit of his stomach, he headed for his study. "We'll make it tomorrow night."

He smacked his forehead and turned back. Where was his mind today?

"Ella, is my tux back from the cleaners? I have an event tonight."

"It's hanging in your wardrobe."

She paled and he read her thoughts as clearly as this morning's newspaper. *The wardrobe where I saw you without a stitch on last week.*

But that was all behind them.

He stole a last look at those legs.

At least he thought it was.

Two

Finished applying her new lip gloss, Ella examined her reflection in the bedroom mirror and let out a sigh.

Life truly could turn on a pin. Only eight months ago she'd buried the poor wasted body of her mother, Roslyn Jacob, who'd finally succumbed to cancer. Later that same day, a man she would revile until the end of time had paid her a visit. A man Ella hoped she would never see again.

She'd first met Drago Scarpini some weeks before the death of her mother. He'd claimed to be her half brother, conceived out of wedlock by Ella's father before he'd married her mother.

Scarpini's own mother, an Italian who'd immigrated to Western Australia many years before, had recently passed away. On her deathbed she'd revealed the name of her son's father, Vance Jacob. Scarpini discovered

that Ella's father had passed away long ago but Scarpini
had wanted to visit his father's widow to see if he had
any brothers or sisters.

A well-packaged story, but from his first, Scarpini
had sent chills up Ella's spine. As days wound into
weeks and Roslyn's condition and faculties deterio-
rated more, Scarpini's visits continued and his ulterior
motives became clear.

Ella had overheard Scarpini talking to her mother
about his difficult life growing up without a father,
without money. Although Vance Jacob couldn't make
recompense now, Roslyn could change her will and
divide the estate between Ella and himself. That,
Scarpini had said, would've made her husband happy.
After all those years of unwitting abandonment, it was
the right thing to do.

Ella had been disgusted at his prodding. Her mother
had been so ill, so confused. And there had been no
proof Scarpini was who he claimed to be. If she'd had a
few thousand to spare, she'd have hired an investigator.

The second time Ella had heard him pushing Roslyn,
she'd told him to get out. Roslyn had died the day after,
sooner than doctors had anticipated. Scarpini had attended
the funeral and had even played the sorrowful, supportive
brother. Later, however, he'd arrived on Ella's doorstep
demanding she divide the estate. When Ella had reminded
him she'd just buried her mother, he'd exploded. He
needed money to pay off pressing gambling debts.

As she'd shut the door in his face, he'd shouted she
would regret it.

The next day, the police had arrived. Scarpini had
alleged Ella had murdered Roslyn with a morphine

overdose to head off the change she had been about to make to her will. It had been an hour of horror Ella would never forget, but, of course, no charges were laid. The following day her front window was smashed and a condolence card left on the mantel. Scarpini had phoned—either she agreed to his suggestion, or he would get nasty. He'd said he intended to haunt her until he got what he deserved.

Quaking all over, she'd immediately called the police, who couldn't do much about Scarpini's threats. She could petition for a restraining order, the officer explained, but perhaps it would be better to wait and see if Scarpini would cool down and disappear. If he physically harmed her, she should get in touch straight away, the officer had advised.

Ella hadn't slept that night. She'd given up her job to care for her mother and, after medical expenses, there was no cash to speak of. The house, as well as an investment property, needed to be sold before the estate could be settled. That would take several weeks, if not months.

By dawn Ella had made two decisions. One, she needed a job to survive until the estate came through. Two, she didn't intend to wait around for Scarpini's next sadistic game. She'd bought a prepaid phone, organized a post office box for correspondence from the will's executor—the husband of a longtime friend of her mother's—and dyed her hair a different shade for good measure. Then she'd applied for the housekeeper's position at the Barkley mansion.

It had been a bold move, particularly without references, but she certainly knew how to cook and clean and do laundry. When she had secured the job, she'd settled and kept very much to herself.

She'd heard nothing from her harasser since. She hoped the police were right and Scarpini had slid back beneath the rock from which he'd crawled. Now with the house and investment property sold and all of her inheritance in hand—just over a million dollars—the time was finally right to take a deep breath, emerge from her cocoon and start afresh.

And what a way to mark the occasion…asked to dinner by the thoroughly enthralling, undeniably dreamy Tristan James Barkley.

Tingling with anticipation, she gazed into the mirror and clipped on her rhinestone eardrops.

She'd lived through a nightmare. How wonderful if dreams could come true…

A knock on her bedroom door made Ella jump.

Tristan's familiar, deep voice reached her from beyond the timber frame. "The reservation's at eight. We need to leave soon."

Swallowing against the knot of nerves stuck in her throat, she called back, "Be right there."

She grabbed her clutch bag then took one last look at her cocktail-length white dress and matching sling-backs. Socialite material? Not even close. But, as Mr. Barkley had said, this wasn't a date. It was a thank-you from employer to employee…infatuated with her boss though that employee may be.

"Ella?"

She blew out an anxious breath. Here goes.

When she entered the kitchen—the room adjoining her own—Tristan's expression opened in surprise then appreciation, and delicious warmth washed from Ella's perfumed crown all the way to her polish-tipped toes.

One corner of Tristan's perfectly sculpted mouth hooked upward as his hands slipped deep into his trouser pockets. "Sorry. I'm still not used to seeing you out of uniform."

Crossing to join him, she fought the urge to smooth the jacket that adorned the magnificent ledge of his shoulders. In an open-neck collared shirt and impeccably tailored trousers, he was tall and muscular and held himself as a powerful man would—with a casual air of authority and an easy yet mesmerizing gaze. She'd always felt so safe here in his house. So appreciated.

As a housekeeper, at least.

She pushed the silly pang aside and straightened her spine. "I'll be back in my uniform tomorrow."

He withdrew his hands from his pockets and moved to join her. "But you really don't like your uniform, do you, Ella?"

No use fibbing. "Not especially."

"My parents' house staff wore uniforms, so I've always provided them, too. But if you'd rather wear regular clothes these last three weeks, I don't know a reason you shouldn't."

Ella's heartbeat fluttered.

Wear above-the-knee hems? Pretty colors? Feminine heels that echoed as they clicked upon these imported marble tiles?

She shook her head. "It wouldn't feel right." Wouldn't feel…appropriate.

"It's up to you, but don't think I'll object." The lines

bracketing his mouth deepened more. "Really, it's not a big deal."

Maybe not to him.

Absurd, but tonight, more than ever, she couldn't help but compare herself to the glamorous sorts with whom Tristan had been pictured in glossy magazines. Eleanor Jacob was an ordinary woman who was destined for an ordinary life. She'd best remember that.

Still, this weekend her relationship with her boss had changed, if only slightly. Soon their association would end and it was likely they wouldn't see each other again. In fact...

She let out a breath.

Heck, maybe he was right. Doing away with her uniform wasn't such a big deal.

She smiled. "If you're sure."

She couldn't quite read the look in his dark, all-knowing eyes before he moved away to check the back door. "I'm sure."

As he rattled the handle, she let him know, "I locked it earlier."

He worked the blinds shut. "Can't be too careful."

It was obvious what lay behind his security consciousness tonight. Her impetuous behavior the day before apparently made him concerned that she might have been harmed in some way.

She apologized again. "I'm sorry about giving you that fright yesterday, Mr. Barkley."

"It's forgotten." But he checked the windows, too.

What must he have thought finding her clothes strewn across the room, her handbag dumped inside out? But she'd had no idea he would return a day early from Melbourne or she wouldn't have donned that swimsuit. Some women didn't mind flaunting their bodies, but she wasn't one of them. She was mortified by the thought of exposing herself to her boss, although he clearly didn't share her reserve.

That day a week ago in his bedroom when he'd turned to face her—muscled, bronzed and breathtakingly bare—he'd seemed surprised by her unexpected appearance, but not the least bit self-conscious. And why the heck would he be, with an amazing body like that?

Tristan left the last window and joined her, his face almost grave. "There's one more thing we need to get straight."

She held herself tight. What had she done now? "Yes, sir?"

"No more *sir* or *Mr. Barkley,* particularly tonight. We don't want to confuse the waitstaff." His dark eyes crinkled at the corners. "Deal?"

Returning the smile, Ella relaxed and nodded.

His hot palm rested lightly on the curve of her arm as he motioned her toward the connecting garage door. He couldn't know the wondrous sizzle his casual touch brought to her blood.

Minutes later, she was buckled up in his sleek black Bugatti, surrounded by the smell of expensive leather and another intoxicating scent—woodsy, masculine, clean. Whenever she changed his bed linen, she was tempted to crawl over the sheets, bundle a pillow close and simply breathe in.

She stole a glance at Tristan's shadowed profile.

What would it be like to have that beautiful mouth capture hers? Be held against his hard, steamy body?

When a bolt of arousal flashed through her, her heart began to pound and her hands fisted in her lap. That kind of make-believe could only get her in trouble. She needed to keep her mind occupied—needed to talk.

Pinning her gaze on the passing pine trees beside the drive, she put a bright note in her voice. "So, how was the function last night?"

The automatic gates fanned open and the European sports car purred out onto the street. "If you want to know, it was boring."

She smiled to herself. No interesting women, then.

She sank back more into the leather. "I thought you were home early."

"You waited up for me?"

When he grinned at her, his dark eyes gleamed in the shadows and her cheeks heated all over again. "I was watching an old movie and heard your car."

She hadn't been waiting up for him. Not really.

"Don't tell me you like those Fred Astaire, Ginger Rogers kind of flicks."

She grinned. "Not that old. Do you remember *Love Story?*" The score of that classic weepie was enough to give her goose bumps.

"I know it. You're a romantic, then?"

"Most women are."

He coughed out a laugh. "You think?"

She blinked over at him. What an odd thing to say. Women daydreamed about meeting Mr. Right. They imagined bouquets and church weddings and sparkling diamond rings. It was usually men who had a hard time committing, particularly when they were so desirable they could enjoy a veritable smorgasbord, Tristan Barkley case in point.

The car pulled up at an elite restaurant, which sat on the fringe of their exclusive Sydney neighborhood. When Tristan opened her car door, Ella asked, "Did you have a reservation already made for tonight?"

It was common knowledge bookings here were as rare as hens' teeth.

He winked. "I said I knew some good chefs."

And she wasn't the least surprised when, inside, the attentive maître d' fairly clicked his heels and showed them to the best table in the house: by an open window with a magical view of the twinkling harbor, secluded from the other guests and a comfortable distance from the live entertainment—a guitarist strumming the soft strains of a ballad.

As the maître d' left them, Ella perused the listed entrées. No prices. She couldn't imagine how expensive each must be.

A waiter nodded a greeting at Tristan as he passed. Tristan nodded back.

Ella lifted a brow. "You obviously come here often."

He kept his eyes on his menu. "Often enough."

She wouldn't ask with whom. Perhaps a different lady each time. He never spoke about the women he dated—she knew only what she occasionally saw in magazines. Tristan Barkley was a brilliant enigma who had yet to lose his heart. Frankly, she couldn't imagine one woman being enough for him. She only had to look into those dark, hot eyes to know he'd be insatiable in the bedroom.

When a vision flew into her mind—naked limbs,

glistening and entwined on his sheets—Ella's heartbeat deepened. She gripped her water glass and took a long, cool sip. This evening would be sweet torture.

They chose their meals—prime steak for him, seafood for her. By the time their food arrived, they'd discussed music, politics and books. He was surprised that she liked mystery novels, too. When he poured their second glass of wine, she realized the nerves in her stomach had settled, almost to the point where she could have forgotten that handsome, intriguing man sitting opposite was her boss.

She was interested to know, "How's your steak?" It smelled delicious and appeared to be cooked to perfection.

He dabbed the corner of his mouth with his napkin. "Almost as good as your filet mignon." She laughed, unconvinced, and his brow furrowed. "It's true." He lifted his wine goblet to his lips. "Must be good not to have to think about the dishes tonight."

"I clean up as I go. It's not so bad with a dishwasher."

"Did your mother teach you to cook?"

"She wasn't much of a hand at cooking, even basics." She gave a weak smile. "That's how I got so good." After her mother's accident eighteen years ago, someone had to take care of those things, she thought.

"Bet your father appreciated your finesse."

Her chest tightened and her gaze fell to the flickering centerpiece candle. "He died when I was ten. A coronary. Heart disease runs in the family."

Tristan slowly set down his glass. "I'm sorry about your dad."

"So am I. He was an exceptional man." She smiled

at a memory. "He taught me to French knit. You wind wool around small nails tacked into the top of a wooden cotton reel and pull the knitting down through the hole—" She cut herself off and, embarrassed, shrugged. "Sounds kind of lame now."

He searched her eyes. "It sounds as if you loved him very much. What did he do for a living?"

"He trained horses. We had stables. Dad got up every morning before dawn, even Sundays. His only vice was betting on the track. Not a lot, but always a few dollars each week."

Perhaps Scarpini had inherited his thirst for gambling.

Ella gripped her cutlery tight. She would not let memories of that man intrude tonight.

"I've never understood some people's need to gamble," Tristan said. "If they thought it through, did the research, they'd understand you lose more than you win."

Her smile was wry. "I think it's more to do with the high when they *do* win."

"Like a drug?"

She nodded.

"You like to gamble?"

She shook her head fiercely. "Not at all."

"I'm sure you've already guessed, neither do I. I only bet on sure things."

His gaze roamed her face and a delicious fire flared over her skin. While she fought the urge to pat her burning cheeks, he poured the last of the wine and changed the subject. "Do you have any brothers or sisters, Ella?"

She inwardly cringed. Not her favorite subject. "It's a matter for debate."

One dark eyebrow hitched. "Sounds intriguing."

"It's a long story."

He pushed his nearly clean plate aside. "I'm a good listener."

She studied him across the table, the encouraging smile, the thoughtful dark eyes, and right or wrong she wanted to share—truly be more than the house staff, if only for a night.

As the waiter cleared their plates, Ella searched for words and the courage to say them.

"I have a half brother."

"Doesn't look as though you approve."

"I have my reasons."

His eyes rested on her, patiently waiting for more.

Did she want to get that familiar with Tristan? she wondered. She was a private person, too. The quiet one at school. The wallflower at the dance. But she wasn't sixteen anymore. She was almost twenty-six and dining with a man she didn't know a whole lot about yet trusted nonetheless. If she was ever going to stretch her wings, now was the time.

Her fingers on the stem, she twirled her glass on the table. "Over two years ago I gave up my job to care full-time for my mother when she was diagnosed with cancer. The disease metastasized to her bones and..." Ella swallowed against the emotion swelling in her throat. "It affected her organs," she went on, "including her brain. Toward the end she sometimes forgot what year it was."

Since her fall down the back stairs eighteen years ago, Roslyn had been "delicate." She'd broken her collarbone and both legs and had lain in a coma for six weeks. Her bones had slowly mended, but her cognitive functions never fully recovered. She'd still been a happy, loving person, just a bit...slow.

A pulse beat in Tristan's jaw. "Taking care of your ill mother...that must've been hard for you both."

At times unbearably hard, watching the person you love most withering away, losing any capacity to care for herself. "Finally she begged me to find a place for her in some facility. I couldn't do it."

His voice deepened. "She was lucky to have you."

When he sat back, she could feel him waiting for the half brother to make an appearance.

She'd thought if she could banish that horrid man from her thoughts, memories of him might fade. She hadn't spoken his name in eight months, but the image of his face was as vivid as the day the police had banged on her door, Scarpini smirking alongside of them.

But rather than bottling it up, perhaps talking about it would help exorcise some of the pain, humiliation and anger she still felt.

She concentrated on the candlelight casting sparkling prisms off her crystal glass. "A few weeks before my mother died, a man showed up claiming to be my father's illegitimate son."

"You didn't believe him?"

That familiar battle raged inside of her. Was he? Wasn't he? Did it make a difference if they were related? she wondered. After the agony Scarpini had put her through, she had no desire to find out.

"He was very convincing..." She thought back. "But I didn't trust his eyes."

"The windows to the soul."

She looked from the candlelight across the table.

Tristan's eyes were clear and filled with unswerving strength and sound purpose.

"Drago Scarpini's were empty. He seemed to look right through me. And his smile…" Icy tendrils trailed down her back and she shivered. "His smile was cold. But he charmed my mother and tried to convince her that my father would want her to acknowledge him now." In a lowered voice, she confessed the rest. "I heard him speak with her about changing her will."

Tristan's chin kicked up. "Sounds as if he was an expert at befriending vulnerable women. A real predator."

"The doctors had given her a few months more to live but she died sooner than expected."

"And Romeo didn't get a slice of the pie."

Her throat constricted. She wouldn't tell Tristan the whole story. He didn't need to hear how she'd been accused of murdering her own mother. It was just too ugly. "After a lot of soul-searching, I decided to gift him ten thousand dollars from the estate."

Tristan looked disappointed. "Ella, you're not even sure you share the same father. Even if you do, he shouldn't have expected anything from your mother's estate."

"My lawyer said the same. But right now I don't have any desire to go through the ordeal of finding out if we are related, and the money was something I felt compelled to give." She half shrugged. "I guess to settle my conscience and be done with it."

There was no right answer, just the memory of her father and what he might have done.

"I'm surprised he hasn't hassled you," Tristan said. "Those types usually don't know when to back down."

A chill crawled up her spine. She had the urge to check over her shoulder, but she shucked it off and instead announced, "It's all in the past now."

The waiter took dessert orders and the rest of the evening they spoke about Tristan's work—the same important project he needed to discuss with the mayor. Ella was sorry when the evening ended and they arrived back home.

As they moved through the garage door into the kitchen, she put her bag on the counter and turned around. Tristan stood close behind her, his expression unreadable, his presence overpowering…his kissable mouth almost too close to resist.

Pressing her palms against her jumping stomach, Ella manufactured an easy smile. "Can I get you anything before we go to bed?"

She withered down to her shoes.

Bad choice of words.

"Thanks, no." His brow pinched. "But there's something I want to ask you, Ella. I have a function to attend next weekend. A black-tie affair. I wondered if you'd like to come."

The flock of butterflies she'd been holding released in her stomach. Was he asking her on a real date? Her? Little Miss Ordinary?

"There's a bigwig in property analysis going," he went on. "I'd like the chance to speak with him in a more relaxed setting, but it's a *couples only* night. Would you mind helping me out? After tonight, I realize you'd make the perfect companion for that kind of thing." He laughed softly. "I'll try not to make it too boring for you."

She closed her parted lips and willed the silly stinging from behind her nose.

So this was a business proposition?

Well, of course it was. Ridiculous for her to think anything else. Next weekend he wanted a date who was polite, presentable and knew her place. A platonic someone who wouldn't interfere with the business he wanted to discuss.

The housekeeper in her glad rags.

But she was being overly sensitive, she thought. Tristan was only being honest and it wasn't as if she had anything better to do.

Her lips curved. "Sure. I don't mind helping out."

"Excellent." He smiled but she glimpsed something else swimming in the depths of his eyes.

No, that was pure fantasy. The only stars in this room were in *her* eyes and she needed to see clearly or she was in danger of being hurt—and it wouldn't be Tristan's fault, but hers for being so silly.

And yet Tristan continued to hold her eyes with his, then his head slanted and he came a step closer. When he reached for her, Ella stiffened and her surroundings seemed to recede and dim. But he didn't kiss her. Rather he touched her left earring, his hand near her neck warming the skin.

His voice was husky, deep. "I've wanted to say all night…these are very becoming."

Could he hear her heart thumping? "They're not real," she managed to say.

"Pity. Diamonds would suit you." His gaze lingered, over her ear, down her jaw, along her trembling lips, causing a fire to flicker up her neck and light her cheeks. For a moment she thought he might lean forward and touch his lips to hers, that he might take her in his arms and kiss her as she'd dreamed so often that he would.

The possibility seemed to hang between them, real and weighted with temptation, but then he merely smiled and moved away.

"Good night, Ella," he said over his shoulder.

She let out her breath on a quiet sigh. "Good night."

She was about to float off to her bedroom when the kitchen extension rang. Tristan had gone, perhaps already on the stairs that led to his bedroom. She'd take a message. Nothing could be that important this late on a Saturday night.

"Tristan Barkley's residence." She waited but no reply. "Hello." Ella frowned. "Anyone there?"

As the clock on the wall ticked out the seconds, in a dark recess of her mind she imagined the hand clutching the other receiver. Had a flash of the face smirking at her irritation.

Slamming the phone down, she tried to catch her sudden shortness of breath. She touched her brow and felt the damp sheen of panic.

But she was overreacting. It was the talk of Scarpini over dinner and the fact the inheritance had come through that had her jumping to conclusions. That call had merely been a wrong number.

Still, before going to bed, she checked the back door—not once but twice.

Three

The following Thursday morning, Tristan swung out from behind his desk to greet his brother, who was striding into the city penthouse suite. Tristan clapped his arms around Josh and they gave each other a hearty hug.

When they broke apart, Josh jokingly tried to spin Tristan around. "Do you ever leave this office? I think you might be growing roots."

Tristan laughed, always happy to see his younger, wisecracking brother, who many people mistook for his twin. "Just because you're in love, doesn't mean the rest of the world grinds to a stop."

Josh's dimples deepened. "You sure about that?"

Tristan pretended to cringe. "Ooh, you have it bad."

"Bad enough to propose."

Tristan's jaw dropped. "Marriage?"

"Even got down on one knee."

Tristan took Josh's hand and shook with gusto. "Congratulations. That's wonderful, just…unexpected. How long have you and Grace been dating?"

Looking every bit the high-powered executive in his tailored business suit, Josh crossed his arms and rocked back on his heels. "Three months and I've never been more certain of anything in my life. Grace and I are meant to be. I can't wait to make her my wife."

Just yesterday it seemed Josh had been captain of the under-nines football team and had scrunched his nose up at girls 'cause they smelled funny. Now he was tying the knot? Tristan ushered Josh over to the wet bar. This news deserved a toast.

He found two glasses. "If you can't wait to exchange rings, I can't wait to welcome her into the family."

For some reason, an image of Ella came to mind—the sound of her soft laughter the other night, the subtle yet alluring scent of her skin. He couldn't remember a time when he'd been more relaxed with a woman over dinner. Guess it was par for the course, given she served him that meal maybe five times a week.

Obviously Ella had enjoyed herself, too, but from day one he'd had the impression she'd be easy to please. After hearing her background, he was more convinced than ever. A loyal daughter who'd cared for her dying mother for years…his respect for her had increased tenfold.

As Tristan reached for his finest Scotch, Josh ran a finger and thumb down his tie. "Welcoming Grace into the family brings me to the second reason for this visit."

Tristan stopped pouring. "You look worried."

"We're having a families' get-together Saturday afternoon. I want you to come."

Handing over Josh's glass, Tristan arched a brow. "Let me guess. What you're *not* saying is you want Cade to come, too."

"Besides the fact Cade and I work together, he is our older brother."

Before taking a sip, Tristan muttered, "Unfortunately."

Josh exhaled. "This feud can't go on forever."

Tristan crossed to the floor-to-ceiling windows and a view of the Opera House shells. The surrounding silky-blue harbor glistened with postwinter sunshine. Narrowing his eyes against the glare, he sipped again, clenching his jaw as he swallowed. "You're too young to understand."

"I'm twenty-eight and I *do* understand that Mum would roll over in her grave if she knew about the rift between you two. You both need to get over it and on with your lives."

"Because what Cade did to me wasn't reprehensible, right?" Tristan's voice was thick with sarcasm. If Josh even knew the half of it…

"If you're talking about the board voting him sole chairman over you not long after Dad's death, Cade offered to continue to share the seat."

If Tristan went along with every decision Cade made. In Tristan's book, that was called chronic egomania. No way could he agree to such terms.

Tristan turned to face Josh. "It was better for everyone for me to decline. The arrangement Dad put into place was never going to work."

He and Cade were to jointly run the largely family-owned Australasian hotel chain. Josh was to be incorporated into the combined chairman's role on his twenty-seventh birthday, which had, indeed, happened last year. If it were only himself and Josh running the show, no problem, they were great friends as well as brothers. But as for the eldest of the trio...

Tristan stared straight through Josh to the imagined figure of his adversary. "Cade and I have never got on," he growled.

Too much competition, only one person willing to budge. As the older brother, Cade had always called the shots, won the praise and Tristan had been expected to smile and follow.

"Profits were down," Josh recalled. "You both had different views on how to strengthen the figures. You wanted to borrow to refurbish the older hotels. Cade said the company couldn't afford the debt. The board agreed."

Tristan deadpanned, "Yet he found the money to buy me out."

"If I remember correctly, you were the one who suggested the split."

"And it was the best decision I've ever made."

He'd examined the refurbishment proposal from every angle and had been certain of its viability. But, once again, Cade had played God.

Tristan knocked back his drink and smacked the heavy glass down on a corner of his desk. The echo reverberated through the room like the fall of a gavel.

He'd gotten out from under the Barkley Hotels' weight and had started a property development company. No more kowtowing to big brother. This recent project would be his largest and most successful enterprise yet—*if* he got the nod on rezoning from Mayor Rufus.

Which brought to mind the other reason Tristan couldn't care less if he ever spoke to Cade again—the fact that Cade had slept with Bindy Rufus while she and Tristan had been dating. Minutes before she'd driven off without him and died in that auto wreck, Bindy had announced to Tristan that she preferred his more mature and wealthier brother.

Talk about a kick in the gut.

Thoughtful, Josh swirled the amber liquid in his glass. "Tristan, there's something else… I'd like you and Cade both to stand beside me when Grace and I say our vows."

Tristan shoved a hand through his hair and tried to laugh. It was either that or cry. "You're not making this easy for me."

Josh's smile was hopeful. "I want us to be a family again. All going well, one day soon you'll both be uncles." He pulled a card from his jacket's breast pocket. "Cade asked me to give you his cell number." He grinned wryly. "In case you'd lost it. He said to call anytime."

Tristan put the card on his desk and changed the subject. They chatted for half an hour and, as soon as Josh was out the door, Tristan found and crushed Cade's card in his fist. Taking particularly careful aim, he shot the wad into the trash basket.

He'd sort out something for the family get-together. He was happy for Josh. In fact, he envied him. Would *he* ever be fortunate enough to find a woman who didn't think of marriage as nothing more than an astronomical weekly allowance with a single child to cement the deal? A woman who wasn't a heartless gold digger as Bindy Rufus had so obviously been.

Ideally, he wanted a woman who was in love with the idea of half a dozen kids and believed in the wholesome riches of "family comes first." Wouldn't it be great if he could simply whip up the perfect wife?

Later that day, on his way through his building to a midafternoon meeting, Tristan passed a jewelry store and an item caught his eye. The price tag was horrendous, but the diamond and Ceylon sapphire earrings would look stunning dangling on either side of Ella's slender neck. The dazzling blue stones matched the color of her eyes precisely.

He walked away remembering the impulse that had gripped him when they'd stood in the kitchen after their dinner out almost a week ago. He'd wanted to bring her near and taste her lips, see how they fitted with his. Crazy stuff. She was his *housekeeper*. Yes, he was looking forward to taking her to the black-tie affair tomorrow evening. She certainly was sexy out of that drab uniform. But she was also a simple, unassuming and honest soul.

He frowned, then slowly smiled.

The perfect wife?

At the dining table that night, Ella poured gravy over Tristan's beef Wellington, feeling his lidded gaze not on the gravy boat but her arm—and inching ever higher. She bit her lip trying to tamp down the tingling sensation radiating from her center. What might happen if, instead of looking, he reached out and touched…?

The instant the thought hit, sizzling arrows shot heat to every corner of her body. She sucked in a breath and stepped back. She'd enjoyed their dinner out last weekend…perhaps a little too much. That time together had fed fantasies she'd secretly dreamed of for eight months. Fantasies about being a rich man's bride.

She held the gravy boat before her, a reminder of her place. "Is there anything else I can get for you?"

His jaw jutted before he nodded, and Ella's heartbeat skipped. Every night that he dined in, she asked Tristan that same question. He'd never once said yes. From the ardent look in his dark eyes now, she knew he didn't want more ground pepper on his potato.

He sat back, elbows on the chair arms, tanned, masculine hands laced over his lap. "Have you eaten yet?"

Worried, she examined his meal. Did something look suspect? "I was about to sit down to mine."

One corner of his mouth lifted. "In that case, join me."

Ella could only blink. She ate in the kitchen or in her room. She'd never sat at this long, polished oak table. Never.

Then understanding dawned. He probably wanted to discuss something he needed from her tomorrow evening. Perhaps he wanted to fill her in on some background of the people attending so there'd be less chance of her feeling out of place. But it didn't really matter what he wanted to discuss. If Tristan had suggested she eat with him, whatever was on his mind must be important.

She backed up toward the kitchen. "I'll get my plate."

When she joined him again, he was on his feet. After arriving home, he'd changed into jeans, the faded ones with the rip in the back pocket that sat like a dream on his lean hips. His white oxford was unbuttoned at the collar, revealing a V of hard chest and dark hair. His jaw was shadowed with daylong bristles that gave him a rugged look. A *sexy* look.

Ella swallowed.

And if she continued along that train of thought, she'd start to drool, which was *not* good etiquette.

He pulled out her chair. Holding her plate firmly in her suddenly buttery fingers, she smiled. "Thank you."

He pulled in his own chair and joined her. "I thought you might enjoy a glass of wine with dinner."

Her gaze skated to a bottle of red next to the condiments. He filled her crystal glass, which he must also have placed there while she'd ducked into the kitchen, then his.

After they'd both sampled the smooth-blend Shiraz, Tristan smiled at her. "Well, this is pleasant. We should have done it sooner."

Ella flicked out her napkin. If nerves weren't pummeling her stomach like a drumroll she might agree. It was very pleasant indeed sitting beside this über-attractive man at his dinner table, surrounded by fine things. The scenario was so unbelievable, she couldn't even have daydreamed about the possibility.

Slipping beneath his sheets isn't in the cards, either, she thought, but she'd daydreamed about that, and more often than usual this week...

"Do you have a gown for tomorrow evening?"

Clearing her throat, Ella fumbled to collect her silverware. "I picked up a dress today." It hadn't been overly expensive. She'd set herself a limit and had very nearly stuck to it. "I hope it's okay."

"I'm sure you'll look stunning."

His eyes crinkled at the corners and flames leapt up from the kernel of heat building low in her belly. He could smile at her like that all day.

"What color is it?" he asked, then tasted the beef and made a groan of appreciation in his throat.

"Kind of a lemony-golden shade."

"It'll go with your hair." Like a touch, his gaze trailed her long, loose braid, which lay over one shoulder, leaving a smoldering line in its wake.

She concentrated to stop her heart belting against her ribs and mumbled, "So the sales assistant said."

His lopsided smile lifted higher before his brows drew together, his gaze dropped and he cut his broccoli, which was bathed in a three-cheese sauce. "Were you going to wear those earrings?"

She remembered his hand near her cheek the other night and the buzz of sexual arousal that had ignited a flash fire over her flesh. She would melt if he ever touched her intimately.

She shook herself. As if that would ever happen. Supermodels. Starlets. Billionaire's daughters—they were the breed of women with whom Tristan normally kept company.

"I'm not sure those earrings will suit," she said, "but if you think I should wear them…"

Eyes still on his plate, he chewed slowly, then with a barely perceivable shrug dismissed it. "Totally up to you."

They ate in silence, Tristan deep in thought, Ella still

coming to terms with the current seating arrangements, until the phone on the sideboard rang.

Ella's midsection turned to ice. She hadn't forgotten that curious phone call the other night. Had it been Scarpini or her imagination working overtime? she wondered. Either way, the phone couldn't simply go unanswered now.

Stomach churning, she rose but Tristan put his hand on her arm. The contact was like the charge of an electric current and her heart catapulted and pounded all the more.

"They can call back," he told her.

The tension locking her muscles eased a fraction and her rubber band legs lowered her back into her seat. Letting it ring out was more than fine with her.

As the phone stopped, Tristan refilled her wine glass.

"The other night made me realize how little I know about you," he said, as if he'd suspected something untoward from her body language. But surely that was only her guilty conscience, she thought.

"There's not much else to tell." She slid her laden fork into her mouth.

"No surprises other than that half brother?"

Nothing he needed to know about. She smiled and chewed, letting him take from that what he would, but he wasn't satisfied.

"No royalty in your background," he joked, "Nobel Peace prizes. No axe murders."

She coughed as she swallowed. "Why would you say that?"

His smile was amused and a little intrigued. "Ella, I was kidding."

She let out her breath. Of course he was. He didn't know about Scarpini's wild accusation of murder. No reason he ever should.

She patted her mouth with her napkin and apologized. "I don't know what's got into me tonight."

"I do. You're preoccupied, thinking about starting a new phase in your life. You'll be missed." He collected his fork and explained, "You've been excellent at keeping every aspect of this place running smoothly."

Her cheeks heated. "You're being kind."

"I'm being truthful." He speared some potato. "I'm surprised no man has snapped you up."

It took a few moments for his words to sink in. He meant marriage. She groaned. "Now you *are* being kind."

His eyes hooked on to hers. "So you've never found the right one?"

For a short time, she'd thought she had—a doctor, Sean Milford. She'd been sadly mistaken. "There's a lot that goes into finding the right one."

"At the top of most women's lists would be a man who can support them."

She slowly frowned. "I'd much rather know I could support myself."

"Even if it meant cleaning houses for the rest of your life?"

Her chest tightened with indignation. What was he suggesting? "I worked in a doctor's surgery before I resigned to look after my mother. I could've found other employment if I'd chosen to. And I certainly wouldn't marry someone because they had money, if that's what you mean."

His smile was genuine. "I didn't think you would. But I wasn't talking about you. You're not most women."

Ella concentrated on his wry expression and it dawned. "You think the women you date are after your bank account?" She laughed. Had he looked in the mirror lately? she wondered. She waved her fork. "You're crazy."

"And you're naive." But his tone said he didn't mind. "So you'd be as happy marrying a plumber as a CEO of a conglomerate?"

"It would depend on which one I loved."

His lips twitched. "Ella the romantic."

"Is there anything wrong with that?"

He smiled that smile. "Quite the contrary."

He'd angled toward her, about to say more, when the phone rang again.

With a growl, he set his napkin aside. "Whoever that is, they're not giving up."

"I'll get it." She pushed back her chair.

Already standing, Tristan put his hand firmly on her shoulder. "Tonight you're a guest at my table. Allow me."

But she sprang up and wove around him toward the phone. "I insist."

He frowned then chuckled as he shook his head. "You're doing a lot of that lately."

She wouldn't have insisted if she weren't worried it might be Scarpini. She didn't want Tristan talking to that man, because it would mean explaining that sordid episode. And in two weeks, she'd be gone from this house for good. Tristan need never know about her visit from the police.

But she'd answered the phone dozens of times this week. No wrong numbers, no heavy breathing. No sign of Drago Scarpini. Nevertheless, her palms were damp by the time Tristan was seated again and she picked up the phone.

"Barkley residence."

Three beats of silence then, "Eleanor? That *is* you, isn't it?"

A concrete wall hit and knocked the breath out of her. She blindly reached for the sideboard and held on.

"If you're wondering how I got the number," Drago Scarpini said, "you can speak with the new receptionist at your lawyer's office. Thank you for the ten grand, by the way. It's a start."

The solicitor's office had given out her number? She squeezed the receiver. "I said under *no* circumstances—"

Ella stopped, but she'd already let slip the acknowledgement Scarpini needed. He was indeed speaking with Eleanor Jacob.

"The receptionist stumbled over herself giving me your number so that a brother and sister could get in touch again." He chuckled. "Some people are just so helpful."

She stole a guilty glance at Tristan, who pushed back his chair again.

"Is everything all right?" Tristan asked.

Her brow prickled as perspiration beaded on her upper lip and nausea rolled high in her stomach. Somehow she managed an unconcerned face, nodded at Tristan then turned and, into the receiver, said very quietly but firmly, "Don't call again."

His laugh was pure evil. "Eleanor, you can run but you can't hide. Not forever, anyway. See you soon, *bella*. Very soon."

As the line went dead, the floor tilted under her feet, like the deck of a ship going under. Her stomach twisted and the light seemed to fade.

Tristan materialized beside her, his supportive arm around her waist. "You're not all right," he said. "Who was that?"

Giddy, she gazed up into his stormy eyes. If she told him that was Scarpini, he'd want to know the rest. She didn't want Tristan to know…

Her father had told her once that mud sticks. In other words, bad opinions are darn hard to shift. Ella believed in being truthful, but in this case she didn't want Tristan for even one moment to picture her as her mother's murderer.

She made an excuse.

"It was a friend wanting to meet me for coffee tomorrow." Her voice was threadbare but not trembling, thank heaven. "I'd already told her definitely not. It would have to be next week."

The lie stuck in her throat. Not only did she hate fibbing, even for this good reason, but linking the word *friend* with Scarpini in any sense made her physically ill.

Tristan's brows nudged together. "You didn't seem pleased to hear from your friend."

Her throat convulsed. "We…have some things to sort out."

"Nothing I can do to help?"

She started to make another excuse, but he held her arms and willed her to look into his eyes. "Let me help, Ella."

She held her breath then crumpled and let the whole story spill out.

"The man who says he's my half brother—Drago Scarpini—that was him on the phone. He phoned a week ago, too, after you'd taken me to dinner that night. He said the money I left from the will was a start. He said he'd see me…see me *soon*. I'd hoped he'd go away, but—"

A bubble of panic caught in her throat.

"Hey, it's okay." Tristan brought her close and rubbed her back. His heat and scent wrapped around her like a warm winter cloak.

When she'd almost stopped trembling, he gently pulled away and looked at her more deeply. "Tell me the rest."

She garnered her strength. Since she'd told him this much, she might as well tell him the rest.

"The day after the funeral the police knocked on my door. They wanted to investigate an accusation…"

When she hesitated, he tipped up her chin with a knuckle. "An accusation of what, Ella?"

She swallowed. "Matricide."

"You?" When she nodded, Tristan laughed. "That's absurd." His amused expression dropped. "What evidence did they have?"

"More or less just Scarpini's accusation."

"More or less?"

"I administered morphine to my mother for the pain.

Scarpini said I overdosed her. I had her prescribed supply but he said, because I'd known a doctor, I could access more."

"What reason could you have for killing your terminally ill mother?"

"Scarpini was livid I hadn't given in to his threats. Whether he'd called the police to intimidate me, or he'd hoped that they'd actually charge me, I don't know. But he told them I was tired of looking after her. That she was about to change her will and I wanted it all."

"The worst kind of gold digger," Tristan murmured gravely.

His pupils dilated until his eyes were burning black coals. When he finally spoke, his voice was dangerously low. "How long have you known this man?"

She was a little taken aback. "I told you. Just weeks before my mother died."

He nodded, but the slope of his brows said he needed to absorb it. Could she blame him? His mind must be reeling.

"Tomorrow," he said, "we'll go to the police."

"No. *Please.*"

She couldn't forget the way the officers had looked at her the day after her mother's funeral, as if, despite the lack of evidence, she was nonetheless a criminal. All those disgusting questions, the sensation of having her heart ripped out and trodden on again. She'd only ever tried to help her mother, yet she would always remember the cold suspicion shining in their eyes.

Mud sticks.

"Ella, this man isn't going to back off without a less-than-friendly nudge."

"I couldn't bear to go through all that again. The questions, the looks, riffling through the details of my mother's illness…"

He studied her pleading gaze for a long moment then nodded once. "It goes against my better judgment…but, all right. Only on the condition that if he calls again, you tell me straightaway. Now—" his hand curved around her jaw, "—I don't want you to worry, okay?"

She eased out a shaky breath. "I'll try."

And she did feel a little better. But the best remedy for worry, she'd discovered long ago, was keeping busy.

Her gaze skated toward the table. She'd lost her appetite and after that episode she wouldn't be much company. "I'll clear the table."

Crossing over, she swept up her plate, then his. When she turned, he was behind her.

He took both plates and set them resolutely on the table. "The dishes can wait. We have wine to finish."

Mere inches divided their bodies but with that call still echoing through her mind…

She touched her clammy forehead. "I think I've had enough wine."

"Are you that eager to get to the dishwasher?"

"No." He grinned at her quick reply and she smiled weakly back. "It's habit, I guess."

"There'll be a dance floor and music tomorrow night." He paused. "Do you dance, Ella?"

She gave him a knowing smile. "You're trying to take my mind off of that phone call."

His head slanted. "Be that as it may…" He waited for her answer.

"I…have danced," she admitted.

With a playful tilt to his mouth, he measured her hesitant expression. "But not recently."

"Seems like a hundred years."

She bit her lip. Too much information.

"Do you know how to waltz?"

She didn't want to make a fool of herself—or him. "I'm really not very good."

"Then perhaps we ought to practice. I can put on some music in the living room." He took a step closer and the edge of his warm hand brushed against hers. "Or we could practice here."

The intercom buzzed, loud and unexpected enough for Ella's stomach to jackknife to her throat. She swung toward the door.

Oh Lord. It was Scarpini wanting in at the entrance gates, she just knew it.

Annoyed at yet another interruption, Tristan groaned and headed for the intercom panel.

"I can get it," she called after him.

"*I'll* get it. And if it happens to be your Mr. Scarpini, I'm more than ready for him."

Ella's knees turned to jelly. Eight months of calm, now the world was spinning out of control.

She straightened and pinned back her shoulders.

Whatever came, be damned if she would stand in the background, quaking in her shoes.

She followed Tristan to the intercom.

"Hello." Tristan waited a beat before one hand clenched at his side. "Hello, who is this?"

The reply was deep and familiar, but not in the way Ella expected. It sounded somehow like Tristan.

"Tristan," the disembodied voice came back. "It's Cade. We need to talk and we need to talk now."

Four

The relief seeping through Ella's system was so wonderfully intense, she almost laughed.

It hadn't been Drago Scarpini buzzing for access at the Barkley gate. As was true of most bullies, Scarpini was a coward, a cockroach. He wouldn't knock on Tristan Barkley's door and expose himself like that, even to get to the person he obviously still viewed as a worthwhile payoff, she thought.

Then Ella saw Tristan's face, his tanned complexion paler than she'd ever seen it. His nostrils flared as he stared at the floor, then he slammed the back of his fist against the wall.

Her stomach muscles clutched in reaction.

"Tristan?" she murmured.

He turned and glared at her as if she were the

enemy. Then he dragged a hand through his hair and his savage expression eased slightly. "Ella, you can clear the table now."

He stabbed a button to open the gates and seconds later a car rumbled up the drive.

Ella let out the breath she'd been holding. Whoever this visitor was, clearly he wasn't welcome. But that wasn't any of her business. She was an employee with a job to do and despite Tristan now knowing her dirty laundry, that hadn't changed.

Running her hands down her sides, she concentrated on slipping back into professional mode. "Would you like me to bring coffee?"

When Tristan looked at her, his eyes were filled with fire—or was that hatred? "He won't be staying that long."

Tristan strode off to answer the front door while Ella calmed her frazzled nerves. What was the visitor's name? Mr. Cade? She started toward the table and with leaden arms collected the dishes, then moved to the kitchen.

She'd never heard that name used in this house. But Tristan had a lot of business dealings to juggle. Sometimes business relationships turned sour. Ella rinsed the dishes while her thoughts churned over Tristan and his visitor, then Scarpini and his phone call.

She dropped her head and cursed the ache in her throat. Oh, how she wished that man would drop off the edge of the planet.

A blind clattered against a kitchen window. Ella's stomach gripped as her concentration snapped up. Her locked muscles relaxed when the scent of coming rain entered the room. Not an intruder, just a storm on the way.

Tristan preferred fresh air to air conditioning, but Ella hurried to close all the windows now, then remembered there were more open in the main living room where she'd vacuumed today.

A moment later, she thumbed on a living room lamplight and went to each window. After checking that the security system was still activated, she spun around and almost tripped over the vacuum cleaner she'd neglected to put away earlier. When she bent behind the settee to bundle up the cord, a man's raised voice permeated Tristan's closed study door.

Crouched behind the settee, Ella froze as her heartbeat boomed a warning in her ears.

Move, Ella. This isn't a position to be caught in.

About to escape to the kitchen, the study door swung open, slamming against the wall.

"Get it through your skull," Tristan snarled, "I will never agree to your terms."

"Never's a very long time," came that other deep and graveled voice.

"As far as I'm concerned, not long enough."

Curiosity won out. Ella peered over the couch and saw her boss speaking with a man. His hair was a shade darker than midnight. He was tall, with a commanding presence similar to Tristan's. The man stood angled toward her. Even at this distance she noticed his eyes, bright yet at the same time seemingly impenetrable…the color of scorched honey. As his gaze narrowed upon Tristan, the amber eyes flashed. But then he slapped his thighs, a gesture of defeat, and stormed away.

Ella slumped as the tension ran from her body. Seconds later, the front door thumped shut. As the echo thundered down the hall, Ella pushed to her feet at the same time Tristan strode past the room and spotted her.

He pulled up, his handsome face dark with fury. She'd never seen him so wild. In fact, other than last week when he'd thought some harm had come to her, Tristan had always kept his emotions well under control.

"Ella," he growled.

She forced her rubbery lips to work. "Yes, Mr. Barkley?" How easily she slipped back to formalities. Suddenly she didn't feel as if she knew him.

Tristan's shoulders came forward, then he closed his eyes and pinched the bridge of his nose. "Would you pour me a drink, please?"

While she beat a path for the crystal decanter on its trolley beside his chess table, Tristan moved into the room and sank into the settee she'd crouched behind. When Ella handed him the drink, he thanked her and knocked back half.

Head back, he concentrated on the ceiling. "You know how you don't like your brother?"

Drago Scarpini? She nodded. "Yes."

"That was mine. How does the saying go? You can choose your friends, but you can't choose your relatives."

She knew Tristan had a younger brother, Josh. But he'd never mentioned anyone named Cade.

A shudder crept up her spine. She wanted to ask what had happened in that room, in their past, for the anger between them to be so strong.

Tristan answered her unspoken question. "Cade wants me to go back and work for the family business."

"Which business?"

He flicked her a curious glance. "Barkley Hotels."

"Your family owns that?"

He leaned forward, holding his Scotch glass between his knees. "I assumed you knew."

He'd never mentioned it, nor had any one of the numerous guests he'd had to the house. Neither had she read anything in the magazines she flipped through.

Looking down, he swirled the liquor in his glass. "I don't suppose you should have. It's been a while since I left the company, and everyone and his dog knows the subject is banned from my ears."

"Because of your brother?"

He eyed her as if she might be withholding some interesting secret. "Sit down, Ella. Here next to me. I need your advice."

She couldn't help it. She laughed. "*My* advice?"

He patted the cushion. "Sit."

She sat. But, even with an arm's length separating them, she felt it—the sexual charge arcing between them like a powerful magnet.

But Tristan seemed oblivious to the sparks and the pull. He was preoccupied with what had transpired in his study moments ago.

He took another sip and let the Scotch sit in his mouth before his Adam's apple bobbed and he swallowed. "My brother's getting married."

"Cade's getting married?"

"Not Cade. Josh. They're as different as day and night. Light and dark. Josh wants Cade and me to mend our fences so we can play happy families at his wedding."

"And that can't happen."

He looked at her as if she'd said something prophetic. "Exactly. I won't forgive and forget."

"Why do you need my opinion?"

"I'd like a woman's point of view. Josh wants both of us to stand beside him when he says I do. I don't want to hurt Josh. But whenever Cade and I are within a mile of each other, volcanoes erupt. If I don't agree, I'll let Josh down. If I do, I'm afraid I'll hurt him even more."

She saw his point. No one wanted a scene at a wedding. "Cade feels the same way?"

"Cade is the eldest. He sees it as his duty to keep the family together, which in his language translates into manipulating everyone to his agenda, including getting me back on board at Barkley Hotels." Tristan huffed over a jaded smile. "You know what beats all?" His eyes grew distant. "I wish things were different between Cade and me. I always have."

Instinctively she reached out and touched his arm. It was an eye-opener to see this vulnerable side to such a masterful man. But it only made her respect him more. He was human.

He loved, even when he thought it wiser not to.

Tristan blew out a weary breath. "It's been one hellova day."

When his gaze found hers, the distance in his eyes gradually crystallized into something here and now, and the kindling that seared down below whenever he was near leapt high. That blush spilled down her cheeks again and she began to push to her feet. She felt uncertain, so out of her depth.

"Ella, don't run away."

Pressing her quivering lips together, she lowered back down. "I thought you might want another drink. And the washing-up's still there—"

"I don't want a drink." The hot tips of his fingers urged her chin higher. "I want to ask you another question. But there's something I'd like to do first."

That was all the warning he gave before he leaned forward and kissed her.

As his slightly parted lips lingered on hers—moist, soft, agonizingly inviting—shock set in at the same time fireworks exploded through her veins. A staggering heartbeat later, instinct took over. A tiny whimper escaped her throat and she leaned in, too.

When his mouth gently left hers, in the shadowed light she saw his dark eyes gleam.

"That was nice," he murmured, their lips all but touching. "We should have done this sooner."

Cupping her nape, he brought her near again, and before she could wonder whether this was good, bad or simply necessary, she submitted fully, her mouth opening to welcome more of his caress, her mind shutting down to everything other than the crazy, magical sensation she'd always known this man's embrace would bring.

Her hand inched up from his bicep, over his shoulder. Uncompromising masculine power. What would the sculpted rock of his body feel like beneath his shirt? What would she give to have him naked now as she'd seen him that morning?

But she wouldn't run from him this time. This time she wanted him close, as close as two human beings could get.

Yet, as the kiss deepened and Tristan's heat and hardness moved in more, Ella saw a flash of Cade Barkley and the emotion changed.

Even a man in control of his world could have an Achilles heel. Clearly Tristan's was his family. He'd been knocked off balance tonight. She didn't want this intimacy to go further simply because he needed to expend some pent-up energy and frustration. She didn't want to surrender this part of herself to serve a purpose that had more to do with Tristan's imminent need to dominate his environment and so much less to do with romance.

Breathless, she dragged herself away and murmured, "I'm sorry."

She couldn't meet his gaze. As desperately as she wanted to, she didn't want to read whatever she might see shimmering in those hypnotic eyes.

His voice was low and rough. "No. I'm the one who should apologize. Like I said, it's been a long day." He pushed to his feet. "We can talk more tomorrow."

As he left the room, Ella's tummy fluttered.

Tristan might have apologized, but he didn't say he wouldn't do it again. And the hunger his kiss had awakened inside of her made her wish he would.

Five

The following evening, Tristan smiled to himself when heads turned as he escorted his date into the prestigious hotel's grand ballroom.

He slid a glance at Ella's profile, radiant in the subdued candelabra light. She wore her golden hair down in long, loose ringlets. The style complemented the serene quality of her bone structure—small straight nose, classic rosebud mouth, a complexion that confirmed good health.

Last night when they'd kissed—softly at first, then with growing passion—he'd lost himself in a moment that had felt so incredibly right. Although he'd pulled back when she'd asked, truth was, now that he'd had a taste, he couldn't wait to have her in his arms again.

After her positive response to his kiss, he was certain

Ella would pay attention to the proposition he had in mind. Sexual compatibility in a marriage was, of course, a necessity. The off-the-scale sizzle factor they seemed to share was a most welcome bonus.

They wove through the glitter and pomp of the highbrow crowd and reached their table. Tristan pulled out her chair, noticing six places at the round table were filled, but two, aside from their own, were still vacant. He took in the nearest place card, Herb Patterson, the man he'd wanted to speak with tonight. When introductions were made around the table, Tristan was told Herb wouldn't be attending.

Ella leaned close to whisper for his ears only, "That's bad luck."

Tristan pulled his chair in more. Perhaps, but he wasn't upset because now he could focus his undivided attention upon the gorgeous woman seated beside him. Remembering that kiss, it was difficult not to sit a little closer, or find some excuse to touch her smooth, tanned skin, or to tell her about the proposition he had in mind—a civilized, sensible arrangement that should suit them both.

Following small talk around the table, which Ella handled superbly, entrée was served.

Above the lilting dinner music, Mrs. Anderson asked, "So, Ella, what do you do for a living? Do you model?"

Ella stopped buttering her bread roll to blink over at Mrs. Anderson. "Me? Model?" She looked as if she might laugh.

"Ella's my housekeeper," Tristan piped up.

Mrs. Anderson coughed on a mouthful of soup. "I beg your pardon? Did you say *housekeeper?*"

Tristan rested his hand on the back of Ella's chair. "Her desserts are heaven on earth."

While Ella's smile said she was a little embarrassed by the attention, Tristan felt nothing but proud. From the expressions on the other men's faces, they wished their help's looks and charm compared. Housekeeper turned perfect special-occasion-partner. If things panned out, she'd become much more than that.

Ella and Mrs. Butler, who'd married a successful dot-com entrepreneur, struck up a conversation that lasted through mains. By dessert Ella was sharing recipes with the other women, who vowed to pass the secrets on to their own cooks and housekeepers. Betty Lipid suggested Ella put together her own celebrity cookbook.

Ella sipped her dessert wine. "I'm hardly a celebrity."

Betty raised a brow. "But our Tristan is." She directed her next words to him. "And might I say, you're looking uncommonly well. All that good living?" She grinned. "Food, I mean."

Tristan didn't take offence. Let Betty Lipid and the others think what they would. In fact, soon he hoped their speculation over himself and Ella being more than employee and employer wouldn't merely be gossip. The more he considered it, the more a proposal of marriage seemed to fit. She was attractive, poised, attentive, demure—he'd bet a bankroll Ella would make a great mother. He'd always envisioned himself with a big family of boys. He wanted to be the kind of dad his father had never been.

He took in Ella's unsuspecting profile and his smile faded.

Her conversation with Mr. Scarpini last night was another reason this idea was a good one. Unless Scarpini was as stupid as he was cowardly, he would quit hassling Ella once he discovered her bystander-employer would soon become her protective husband.

Ella pushed away her mousse and held her stomach. "Delicious, but I can't eat another bite."

Tristan set his napkin on the table. "I'm done, too."

When he stood and took her hand, a look of terror filled her eyes. "What are you doing?"

"They're playing our song."

He tugged and she reluctantly got to her feet. "We don't *have* a song."

"We do now."

A step behind, she followed him out onto the dance floor. When he wound his arm around her, she stiffened, but as they began to move, her rigidity dissolved bit by bit. Positioned against each other like this, his body pressed lightly against her supple curves, he knew she was thinking about their kiss. So was he. He couldn't wait to sample those honeyed lips a second, then a third time.

But he could wait…at least until he got her home.

"Have you spoken to your brother?" she asked.

Tristan frowned. If she'd wanted to temper his mood, it worked.

"No, we haven't spoken," he replied. "But I'll need to, I suppose. Josh is holding a get-together tomorrow with his fiancée and her family. Cade will be there."

Her grin was wry. "Good luck."

Tristan's palm traveled to the dip in her back. "Would you like to come?" he asked, swaying with her, enjoying the up close and personal contact more than she could know. With her alongside him, the family ordeal with Cade present wouldn't seem half as unpleasant, which was a bit of a revelation. He'd never felt so assured about a woman's company before.

"Are they needing someone to serve?" she asked innocently, and he laughed.

"No, Ella, I want you to accompany me."

She blinked and her sapphire eyes sparkled. "How will you explain me?"

He played with a frown. "How *should* I explain you?"

She trod on his toe and they both flinched. "How about as the woman who can't dance to save herself?"

"You have other talents. You don't need to dance well."

She huffed good-humouredly. "At least you're honest."

"Not insensitive?"

"I can't imagine you ever being that."

Her lashes lowered and he gathered her slightly closer, smiling at the same feeling he'd experienced when he'd hired her months ago. This—*she*—felt right. Last night when he'd gone to bed, he hadn't been able to shake the image of how good she'd looked in that pink bikini. Then the bikini had vanished and he'd imagined them together in his bed. The more he thought about it, the more he wanted it. Wanted her.

With his mouth resting against the shell of her ear, he murmured, "You look stunning in that gown."

After a moment, she replied in a thready voice, "Thank you."

"But you didn't wear your earrings."

He deliberately brushed his lips against her ear again and smiled as a tremor ran through her.

"I'm afraid they wouldn't pass the 'are they real or not' test."

He grinned. Yes, those sapphire drops he'd seen in the jewelry shop window would have looked perfect tonight. But perhaps Ella didn't like sapphires. Some women preferred emeralds, others wanted only diamonds. He'd known a few women like that. "Do you have a favorite stone?"

"A gem, you mean? I've never thought about it."

He heard the note of strain and uncertainty mixed with brewing arousal in her voice and realized how much pressure his palm had exerted on her lower back. He was aroused too, and Ella, as well as the area above her thighs, would no doubt have recognized the fact.

Not feeling nearly as contrite as he should, he said, "I'm making you uncomfortable." She accidentally trod on his foot again. Hiding a wince, he pulled back and cleared his throat. "Would you prefer to sit down?"

Her face was pained. "I think *you* would."

He chuckled and admitted, "Next time I'll wear steel-toe boots."

"You're a sucker for punishment."

"It's no hardship, believe me."

No truer words had been spoken.

He wasn't quite conscious of the movement, but as he smiled into her eyes, his head bowed over hers until her spine arched slightly back. He felt her intake of air and saw in her eyes... She wondered if he would kiss her again, here in front of everyone. And, God above, he was tempted.

Instead he found the strength to show some mercy and release her. On their way back to their table, they bumped smack-dab into Mayor Rufus.

Hiding his surprise—he wasn't prepared for this meeting—Tristan squared his shoulders. "George. I didn't realize you'd be here."

They shook hands and the mayor nodded once. "Tristan. Nice to see you." But the mayor's tone wasn't convincing.

Tristan set his jaw. He'd invested not only large amounts of money, but also his heart and soul into his current resort project. This man could seal the deal with a nod on rezoning, and just as easily run a red pen through and obliterate twelve months of Tristan's working life—geological reports, feasibility studies, copious meetings with architects.

Did Rufus still blame Tristan for his daughter's death? If he knew the entire story, perhaps Rufus would understand. Although the temptation was there, Tristan couldn't consciously tarnish Bindy's memory or scandalize his own family name, though Cade hardly deserved his loyalty.

The mayor turned to Ella. "I don't believe I've had the pleasure."

Tristan made the introduction, knowing Rufus would be remembering a time when his daughter had been the woman on Tristan's arm. "George Rufus, this is Ella Jacob."

The mayor smiled. "Are you new to town, my dear? I don't believe I've seen you at similar events."

"Ella works for me," Tristan said. The mayor would have discovered as much when he arrived for dinner in two weeks' time.

The mayor nodded as if that made some sense. "Personal assistant?"

"Housekeeper," Ella admitted.

The mayor's brow creased before his face lit up. "So you're the young lady who bakes a caramel apple pie to die for?"

Ella lifted a modest shoulder. "I've received a few compliments on that recipe."

"I'm looking forward to adding to those compliments. I presume Tristan told you I invited myself over for dinner?"

She smiled. "I'm planning something extra special."

"But caramel apple pie for dessert?"

"With your choice of cream or warm brandy custard."

The mayor chuckled. "I'll look forward to it." His smile tightened. "I hope Mr. Barkley is taking good care of you." He redirected his attention to Tristan.

Tristan inwardly cringed. Ella didn't know the full implication behind the mayor's words. But if he decided to take this relationship to the next level, Tristan supposed he'd best tell Ella the whole sordid story. He hadn't pushed Bindy Rufus toward her untimely death. She'd chosen her own path, which included infidelity with the worst possible partner.

A photographer with rumpled hair and an ill-fitting suit interrupted them. "Mind if I get a shot for the celebrity page?"

Tristan acquiesced and after some minor staging, the flash went off. Seemed he, Ella and the mayor would share the limelight somewhere in tomorrow morning's print.

The mayor bid them good-night and, back at the table, Ella stifled a yawn.

Tristan studied her face. He should have noticed earlier the shadows under her eyes. "You're tired."

"No, I'm not," she replied too quickly.

She didn't want to spoil his night. Sweet, but it suited him to leave. Now that he'd made up his mind, he didn't want to delay moving forward.

He was serious about pursuing the marriage-of-convenience proposition. For Ella it would mean a stable husband with the resources and temperament to treat her well. He in turn would have a wife other men would envy—the veritable girl-next-door with no pretences or ulterior motives. No headaches. No heartache.

Tristan's good humor dipped as he swept his jacket off the back of his chair.

Ella's naiveté was all the more reason to keep an eye on Cade tomorrow. His older brother had white-anted him before. No reason to trust him now.

He collected Ella's purse from the table. "It's almost eleven," he said, handing the purse over. "Time to call it a night."

Her eyes unwittingly flashed with gratitude before she shrugged. "Well, if you're sure you're ready."

Tristan smiled at his beautiful companion. He was more than ready.

During the drive home, Ella was floating.

She'd never attended an event quite like tonight's. Those people were some of the wealthiest in the state—in the *country*—but despite having had next to no sleep last night, she hadn't made a social blunder. The reason was clear. Her companion.

She looked across at Tristan sitting relaxed behind the wheel, his expression intent as the night shadows flickered over his classic profile.

He'd been the perfect escort, making her feel not only beautiful but...*special,* even when she'd trodden on his foot, not once but twice.

Ella dropped her gaze to her hand holding her knotting stomach. The night wasn't over yet. More than instinct whispered to her what was in store. Tristan planned to kiss her again. She saw it in his eyes and the tilt of his mouth whenever he smiled at her.

He'd obviously thought more about last night's embrace and wanted to test those waters again. What else did he have planned? How much was she prepared to give? she wondered. What exactly did Tristan want from her?

Possibly a brief interlude with an employee who would be out of his life in two weeks. Fulfillment of a curiosity with no lingering ties. Surely nothing more than that.

As Tristan drove into the garage, Ella tried to divert her thoughts. The dinner she intended to prepare for the mayor seemed a good topic.

"Do you know of anything special other than pie the mayor would like served?"

"Actually he's a big fan of clam chowder. His wife served it whenever I shared a meal with the family."

As Tristan shut down the engine, Ella unsnapped her seat belt. "I didn't realize you two were that close."

"Not anymore." He opened his car door. "Some time ago, I dated Belinda Rufus."

Ella looked hard at him. No mistaking such a unique last name. "The mayor's daughter?"

He nodded, then got out of the car and rounded the vehicle to escort her inside.

"We'd been seeing each other for three months," he continued, thumbing on the kitchen lights. "She died in tragic circumstances—a car wreck."

Ella was taken aback. "I'm sorry, Tristan."

He nodded then added in a low voice, "The mayor blamed me."

"Were you driving?"

He shook his head and leaned on the back of a kitchen chair. "I'd invited Bindy to a friend's wedding. Not far into the reception party, it was clear she'd had far too much champagne. When I suggested we leave, she stumbled out onto the balcony. The fresh air only made her intoxication worse. She must have known I wasn't impressed, but she wouldn't stop. I thought she was talking nonsense at first, and then she told me—" His Adam's apple bobbed, then he cleared his throat and scrubbed his jaw. "She said she'd slept with Cade the week before."

Ella fell back against the bench. "But why?"

"She seemed to take relish in the fact that Cade was the wealthiest of the Barkley brothers."

"Oh, Tristan. No wonder…"

"Although she obviously expected me to, I didn't explode. Instead I had this perverse urge to laugh." He sneered. "Big brother Cade was at it again."

She couldn't imagine feeling so betrayed. Scarpini might be her half brother—if, in fact, that were true— but Tristan had known Cade all his life. They'd grown up in the same house, shared the same parents. How could brothers turn out so differently? She hadn't known Tristan long, but instinctively she knew he would never act so appallingly.

He shrugged and pushed off the chair. "Perhaps Bindy wanted a duel at dawn. But it only crystallized what I'd been feeling more and more. We weren't right for each other and that confirmed it." Deep into his thoughts, he moved toward her. "Bindy stumbled away. A minute later I saw my car speed off. She'd had my keys in her bag. I followed in a friend's car, but…"

Ella continued for him. "She crashed."

He blinked then nodded once. "She died instantly." He took a deep breath and rubbed his forehead. "The mayor blamed me. Said I didn't take care of his little girl. He thought I'd tried to dump her and had broken her heart." A corner of his mouth pulled down. "What a joke."

So that's what the mayor had meant by that comment, *I hope Mr. Barkley is taking good care of you.* She'd thought his tone, if not his words, had seemed off at the time.

"What did the mayor say when you told him the truth?"

Tristan rolled back one shoulder and lifted his chin. "I didn't say anything. Bindy was dead. Nothing would come from discrediting her name to her father or anyone else."

"And Cade? What did he say when you confronted him?"

His jaw flexed. "We didn't discuss it."

"Never?"

Tristan's right hand fisted by his side. "Cade knows

what he did. What he *always* does. He thinks about himself. I have no desire to rehash it."

"But if Bindy was drunk…" Ella shrugged. "Well, maybe she got confused."

His smile was a sneer. "She wasn't confused about Cade's appendix scar or the 'cute' tick at its lower end."

She guessed scenarios such as this played out in real life more than people would like to admit, and not only among the rich and famous. Money and sex had the potential to warp people. Sometimes destroy them.

"And now you have to face Cade at this get-together," she said.

"I'll do it, but only for Josh's sake. And I'll behave. Hopefully Cade will, too."

He looked at her then as if there might be a deeper meaning to his words and she wondered. Surely it wasn't mistrust of *her* clouding his eyes.

They weren't a couple, and even if they were, she would never cheat as Bindy had done. If things weren't working out between two people who weren't married it was better to sever the relationship than continue to hurt each other. She'd followed her own advice when she'd called off her relationship with Sean. Apparently he'd never thought her good enough in any case…

Ella pushed away the ghosts from her past. That was all so long ago. Like Tristan, she didn't enjoy revisiting the less memorable pages of her personal history. And, remarkably, Tristan's skeletons competed with hers. They'd both been accused of killing a person they cared about.

Tristan moved closer. "Ella…there's something

else I feel we need to discuss." His gaze probed hers. "It's about us."

Her insides tensed as a thread of panic wound through her. Tristan was going to bring up that kiss. But after the emotion of that conversation—his being with another woman and her untimely death—she wasn't ready to go there, even to discuss it.

Curling some hair behind her ear, she slid her foot back toward her bedroom door. "Do you mind if we talk in the morning?" She gave him a weak smile. "I'm more tired than I realized."

His earnest expression deepened before he nodded and said, "Of course."

She slid back her other foot and smiled. "Great. Well…good night. Thank you for tonight."

He seemed about to say something more, then only nodded again. "My pleasure. Sleep well."

But Ella didn't sleep well. Anything but.

After tossing and turning for what seemed like hours, she wandered out to the dark kitchen for a glass of water. With her hand on the refrigerator door, she heard a shuffling noise, then a rustle. Her stomach pitched and she went cold all over. A light was shining down from further in the house, possibly the library. Then she heard stealthy footsteps on the tiles.

When Tristan appeared, she released a tension-filled breath at the same time their eyes connected in the shadows. He stopped dead before a warm smile spread across his face and he moved toward her.

One part of her wanted to retreat to her bedroom— she was dressed in a negligee, without a wrap. But the room was filled with forgiving shadows, and the air surrounding them was suddenly heavy with curiosity.

When he stopped before her, silver moonlight shining in through the window highlighted his broad, bare chest. The masculine scent of his body filled her lungs. How she loved that smell.

"You can't sleep?" His voice was a deep rumble that resonated through to her bones.

"Not a wink," she admitted.

"Me, neither." He slanted his head on a teasing smile. "Maybe we shouldn't sleep together."

She looked into his eyes and knew what he was suggesting—the exact opposite. She couldn't deny that the idea of sleeping together was frighteningly appealing.

As the seconds ticked by, the space separating them seemed to compress and at the same time stretch an agonizingly forbidden mile. Did she want to breach that space? The stillness of his towering frame told her that Tristan only needed her nod.

She quivered inside.

Should she?

Shouldn't she?

She wet her dry lips. "Tristan?"

"Yes, Ella?"

Her throat convulsed and she swallowed. "You want to kiss me again, don't you?"

His smile changed. "Yes, I do." He moved closer until his body heat seemed to meld with hers. "And I think you want me to."

Quivering again, she stepped away from her safety net and nodded. "Very much."

Six

When Tristan drew her close and his mouth covered hers, Ella gave herself over to a tingling tidal wave of pure pleasure. After the anticipation of wondering these past twenty-four hours, Tristan's kiss tonight was even more than she remembered—better than heaven, as if that should be a surprise.

As the strong band of his arms urged her closer still and he expertly deepened the kiss, she could have passed out from the blistering sensual overload. So many times she'd contemplated enjoying the intimate attentions of this powerfully attractive man. People were naturally drawn to and admired his superior bearing. Why should she be any different? She was only human, even if tonight *he* felt like a god.

Tristan's palm spread and pressed low on her back

as his other hand cradled and almost imperceptibly turned and kneaded the back of her head. Trembling inside, Ella clung to his chest, reveling in the musky scent of pure male and feel of flesh-and-blood granite. Such a moment should last an eternity, but now that they'd started, Ella wanted more.

More of what she'd glimpsed that day in his bedroom.

When Tristan reluctantly broke the kiss, he scooped her up in his arms and Ella's breath left her lungs in a soft exclamation of surprise. His heavy-lidded eyes lingered on her lips as he began to move out of the kitchen, toward the stairs…

The stairs that led up to his bedroom.

At a jab of alarm, her eyes must have rounded because he stopped abruptly and blinked twice. "I'm moving too fast," he said.

There was little doubt what he would expect when they arrived upstairs. And she was certain that's where he was taking her. In truth, wasn't a night in each other's arms what she'd dreamed of experiencing, too? It'd been so long since a man had held her, and this wasn't just any man. If that was Tristan's intention—to make love to her without reservation—shouldn't she grab the opportunity, as well as the memories that would last a lifetime? This wasn't a case of Tristan merely needing to expend some energy. Regardless of what happened after tonight, right now he truly wanted her as a woman.

And she wanted him, too.

Her tummy fluttered as she looped her arms around his broad neck.

"I'm game," she murmured, "if you are."

His eyes widened as if he were almost taken aback by her reply, but then his expression softened. "I'm more than game." He began to walk again.

"If we're awake at midnight you can wish me happy birthday."

"It's your birthday tomorrow?"

"I'll be twenty-six."

He smiled that sexy smile. "Then I guess we have some celebrating to do."

She crossed her ankles and sucked in a decisive breath. "I could whip up a cake." She liked chocolate torte, but Black Forest with lots of cherries was his favorite.

Holding her tighter, he mounted the stairs two at a time. "I don't want you in the kitchen, Ella. I want you in my bed."

They crossed the threshold into his room. The butterflies in her stomach went berserk when he flicked on a lamplight and the tawny satin coverlet and ruby-colored cushions of his king-size bed materialized out of the dark. She'd smoothed his sheets hundreds of times and had wondered about stretching out on them just as often. Difficult to believe that tonight her fantasies would finally come true.

He set her on her feet and his warm, steady hands slid down the sides of her satiny nightgown.

"This is nice." His mouth lowered to sample the curve of her neck.

She angled her head, shivering as she gave him better access. *Nice?* Was he referring to their new situation or her negligee? she wondered.

"I bought it the same day I picked up my evening gown."

Her voice sounded thick as his teeth slowly danced down her throat, making her flesh tingle and nipples bead tight. When her fingers found his head and flexed longingly in his hair, she felt his smile on her skin.

"Do you always wear this kind of thing to bed?" he asked. "Or were you hoping we'd bump into each other tonight?"

"I usually wear button-up pajamas."

His raspy jaw grazed as he kissed an adoring line of fire up her throat. "Tonight it's difficult to imagine you in anything other than French silk."

Through the haze of building desire, a vague sense of self-consciousness sparked. She wasn't like the women with whom he usually kept company. She wasn't at all…refined. "I don't normally buy silk negligees or spend a lot on perfume or jewelry."

"Then maybe it's time someone did for you."

His sultry admission threw her. But before she could think more on it, he found the bow at her cleavage and tugged the ribbon loose. Then he cupped her shoulders and, with a sculpting movement, dragged down the thin straps of silk.

The negligee slipped into a soft puddle around her feet. She sucked in a breath at a kick of raw, physical need as he brought her close, his long, muscular legs creating a V either side of hers. His rumbling tones resonated through her as his hands massaged her upper arms, drawing her up and toward him. He tasted the slope of her shoulder as if she were a fine delicacy.

"Is this okay?" he murmured against her skin.

Dissolving into him, she sighed on a delicious shiver. "*Okay* isn't the word."

His slightly roughened hands combed down her arms, detouring over her rump to scoop her in and up. Her breath caught.

He was so hard.

He took a seductive, lingering kiss from the corner of her mouth. "You're perfect."

If he hadn't been holding her, Ella would have swayed. And she could barely breathe. Every bubble of oxygen had been consumed by the fire raging inside of her.

He kissed her again—thoroughly this time, until her head spun and limbs floated away. When he left her lips and looked into her eyes, his gaze was hot and purposeful.

"Ella, I want you."

Her body tensed as trapped air burned in her lungs and stars began to dance in her head. The reality of having Tristan Barkley kissing her, telling her he *wanted* her, was overwhelming, almost too much to absorb.

His knuckle nudged her chin up and he searched her eyes. "Remember, if I'm going too fast, we can take it slow—as slow as you want to go."

She tried to even her breathing, to grasp what was happening and accept it. "Tristan…I…I…"

He blinked several times then let out a breath and pressed a kiss to her brow. "It's okay. You don't have to say it. It's too soon." He smiled as his gaze roamed her face. "Let's get you dressed."

Dropping onto his haunches, he found her negligee

at her feet. She wanted to pull him back up, tell him he was mistaken and then lock her lips with his again. But she stilled when his hands slid up her legs as he towed the fabric along. Halfway up, when he reached her hips, his progress stopped.

His warm breath lingered on her thighs, high where her legs joined and a hypersensitive spot had picked up on the heat of his mouth and had begun to beat and glow. She was agonizingly aware of how damp her panties were—how desperately, shamelessly, she wanted him to touch her there. If he did, she just might explode.

Like a warm, soft breeze, his mouth brushed her navel and a whimper of longing escaped from her throat.

"I don't mind you being shy, Ella. But I want you to know you don't have to be. You're beautiful." His mouth brushed again and his hands slid higher to hold her hips. "Just…please, give me a moment," he groaned, "then, I promise, I'll let you go."

He didn't wait for permission this time. Instead he tasted long, moist kisses that led down from her belly to her panty line. The warm tip of his tongue trailed back and forth just below the elastic as his fingers dug gently in, angling her hips even more toward his skilled mouth.

Tipping back her head, Ella sighed as her hands drifted to his hair. Tristan thought she was beautiful. He'd asked if she wanted to make love. And with every word—every wondrous graze of his lips—she wanted him more and more.

She was about to surrender all when his mouth left

her burning flesh. Pushing to his feet, he towed the negligee up with him, replacing the straps over her shoulders.

Ella exhaled as a chunk of her sizzling tension fell away. But she wasn't ready to let that feeling go. She wanted that scorching, drugging heat to continue. She wanted his mouth on her again, but this time she wanted it *everywhere* and all at once.

She cupped his stubbled jaw in two hands and willed him to see the depth of the need in her eyes.

"Make love to me," she whispered.

His brows knitted then his expression changed in a way that made her feel all the more desired. A way that made her simmer then burn. He studied her for a long, super-charged moment.

And took her hand.

He led her to his bed, ripped back the covers then sat on the edge of the mattress she'd covered with fresh, fragrant sheets that morning. Standing before him, she dropped her negligee then he slipped her panties off her hips, down her thighs. When she stepped out of the scrap of silk and stood before him completely naked, she felt at once released, totally free and at the same time incredibly vulnerable.

His warm hands on her waist drew her toward him, twirling her as he brought her down onto the cool sheets so that she lay on her back, partly captured beneath him.

His smile flashed in the shadows. "We'll toast your birthday with French champagne at midnight."

A tantalizing thrill rippled through her. "I like the sound of that."

Two fingers wove up the inside of her thigh. "I like the *feel* of this."

He proceeded to show her how much.

He caressed her body from head to toe, and with so fine a skill she wondered whether she would ever descend from the clouds. When she was beyond ready, when her breasts were on fire and her core screamed for sexual release, he found a condom in his side drawer, then, dotting meaningful kisses on her brow, he gently nudged in.

The breach stole her breath away. Yes, it had been a long while, and she hadn't had many sexual partners, but this…

This sensation was beyond anything she'd ever dreamed.

As her lips parted to take in more air, she opened her eyes and looked up into his dark, appreciative gaze.

"Relax." His voice was low and husky. "I don't intend to rush."

With the deep, steady thrum of his words drifting through her, his knee edged hers out a little farther, then he began to move with such a beguiling, animalistic genius, soon she couldn't remember a time before this. Before *them.* Her fingers trailed over the damp rise of his broad back and some insane part of her wanted to hold on—past tonight, into tomorrow and right the way through to next week and next year.

A few delicious moments later, all thought vanished in a blast of steam as an inferno gripped her low and wonderfully deep inside. Holding on to his hips, she cried out and clamped down around intense, raw pleasure—bright, throbbing, exploding sparks. Radiating waves pulsed through her, drawing another gasp from her lips, making her soar far away from any worry or doubt she'd ever had. She'd never felt more alive.

As the divine waves slowly ebbed, every muscle in his body locked above her. Her hands wove up between them, her touch reveling in the brute strength of his chest and his neck. She welcomed his final thrusts—his deep groan of pleasure and release—at the same time a serene knowledge settled over her.

This was what it was like to know a real man's love.

She wanted to know it again.

The next morning, Ella awoke feeling as if she were still in a dream. Lying on her side in the darkened room, she opened her eyes to a sliver of daylight spearing through a crack in the blinds. The air was still, the mattress soft, and on her skin—in her hair—she smelled him.

As sensual remembrances cascaded through her mind, Ella touched her lips. Her mouth still burned from his penetrating kisses. Her body glowed from a night that had been the most wondrous of her life.

A ball of nerves bunched high in her stomach.

Now it was morning. Was she still Tristan Barkley's lover, or was she back to being the maid?

Bringing the sheet with her, she carefully rolled over. Sound asleep, Tristan lay on his back beside her. One hand cradled his head on the pillow; his other arm was sprawled out at a right angle to his side. She could testify that his abdomen was indeed as rock solid as it looked. So were his biceps and barreled chest, which rose and fell in the steady rhythm of his slumbered breathing. A bristled shadow darkened his square jaw. His full lower lip was relaxed and frighteningly tempting.

He looked totally at peace, and every cell in her body begged her to wake him with the touch she now knew he liked best.

She fought the urge. They'd been up past dawn. He needed sleep. Then he'd need breakfast. She'd start with hash browns.

She eased away from him, but before her toes met the soft carpet, a hot hand caught her wrist.

"Where do you think you're going?"

Her attention shot back around. At the same time she saw his smile flash, he pulled her down. Her respiratory rate doubled as his fingers funneled through her hair and he brought her mouth to his.

When he deigned to release her, flushed with fresh arousal, she relaxed upon the plateau of his hard chest.

His eyes twinkled into hers. "Happy birthday."

Fully in his thrall again, she sighed. It was the best birthday in the history of the world.

"Are you hungry?" she asked.

"What's on the menu?"

"Hash browns and eggs."

After pretending to consider it, he frowned. "I don't think so."

She sat up, taking with her some sheet as a cover. "How about pancakes?"

"With maple syrup?" She nodded, but he shook his head. "What else can you offer?"

"Anything you want."

His expression sobered. "I'll have you."

A swell of emotion brought moisture to her eyes.

After eight months of fawning and only one night of passion, this couldn't be love. The overwhelming need to know his heat and masculine power against her…to hear the hypnotic rumble of his voice…

No, this couldn't be love, but it was something pretty close to it.

When he moved to collect her in his arms again, his gaze hooked to the right…to the clock on the side table. He cursed, and when she saw the time she knew why.

"When is the family get-together today?" she asked.

He fell back onto the pillow and groaned. "Too soon for me."

She lay back down facing him. Her hands beneath her cheek on the pillow, she surveyed his grave profile—his straight nose, the proud, jutting chin.

"Maybe Cade won't show up."

"Not his style," he said. "From the time he could talk, he needed to be the center of attention. Kingpin. At football, at studies…"

At women?

Her next words were a whispered thought that slipped out. "You'd never be second best to me."

When he darted her a surprised then thoughtful look, she wanted to add that she'd never meant anything more in her life.

She sucked down a breath.

Time to move before she said something really incriminating.

She sat up again. "I'll fix breakfast."

"You like taking care of people, don't you?"

She stopped and gave a mental shrug. "I guess so."

"Your mother, even before she was ill?"

She looked hard into his knowing eyes. How could he have guessed? Had it been her comment about her mother not coping with cooking?

"My mother had a bad fall when I was quite young," she explained. "Her physical injuries healed, but her mind stayed slightly impaired. She didn't cope very well after my father died. I helped where I could."

Moments before he'd passed away, her dad had asked Ella to look after her mother. She'd have done it anyway. Roslyn Jacob had been a good mother, just…disorganized, which was kinder than the things some people had whispered behind their backs.

Tristan reached to curl some hair behind her ear. "It's time someone took care of you."

Ella blinked as emotion rose in her throat. If she wasn't looking after someone else's needs, at the very least she was looking after her own. The idea of being cared for, rather than caring for others, was a concept she couldn't fully form in her mind. It was too…*not her*.

And yet, how wonderful if it could be.

His lazy smile broke the moment. "Before we do anything else, let's have a soak."

Mmm, what a nice idea. "You want me to run the tub?" His bathroom was an imported marble paradise, the spa bath more a small pool.

"I'll let you pour in the bubbles," he promised, running a fingertip down her arm, "if I can scrub your back."

"Just my back?"

He mimicked her teasing grin. "Already you know me so well."

Then, to prove his point, rather than leaving the bed, he brought the sheets up way over their heads.

Seven

An hour later, fresh from the spa bath, she and Tristan were in his car and on their way to his brother's house. It wasn't far into the trip before Tristan announced he needed to make a quick detour.

After parking, he ratcheted on the handbrake and turned to Ella.

"I need to grab something." He snatched a kiss from her cheek and smiled. "Won't be long."

She inwardly sighed at the tingling effect his kiss left behind. "I'm fine. Take your time."

She didn't mind the time alone. In fact, she'd take every minute she could to get her mind around what had happened last night...and this morning. Had she really spent such an unbelievable night with Tristan Barkley, her boss? Every time she closed her eyes, she relived the euphoria of their lovemaking. What would tonight bring?

Settling into her seat, Ella let her eyes drift shut.

Tristan hadn't been gone a minute before her car door swung open. She sat up, expectant.

"Well, will you look who it is."

Ella's hand flying to her mouth didn't muffle the sound of her gasp. Her pounding heart felt in danger of leaping from her chest. "What are you doing here?"

Drago Scarpini laid a forearm over the door window and leaned in. "Catching up with my long-lost sister." His grin was a leer. "Long time no see, sis."

The scent of his cheap aftershave worked on her senses like salts and Ella's fright turned to sickened anger. "You followed us?"

He ran an eye over the luxurious interior of the Bugatti. "Wealth becomes you."

Her chin lifted. "I suggest you leave. My boss will be back any minute."

"Your boss. Yes. I've done some checking. You started work for Tristan Barkley when you disappeared off the face of the earth eight months ago. You're his housekeeper." He raised a thick black brow. "Although, from the look, you're a little more than that. Housekeepers don't passenger with their employer on Sunday mornings." She didn't notice the newspaper until he bent back a page and held it under his chin. "And they don't wear evening gowns and rub elbows with mayors when they work." His menacing eyes gleamed. "You've gone and landed yourself a whale, haven't you, Eleanor?"

Her fingers dug into her lap but she kept her voice

low and amazingly calm. "You don't know what you're talking about."

He pulled up straight. "I'm talking about you saving us both a lot of agony and agreeing to share some of your good fortune." The twisted smile fell from his face. "My patience is running thin."

Five minutes after Tristan had entered the jewelry store tucked inside his building's lobby, he left with an unmarked packet in his hand and a ripple of anticipation coursing through his veins. He'd bought two birthday gifts for Ella—a gold pen set to autograph that bestselling cookbook when it came out and those earrings.

He'd thought about buying a diamond ring to present to her when he put forward his proposal. Last night and this morning had only validated what he'd already known. She'd make the perfect wife and hopefully he was something near what she had in mind for a husband. She couldn't deny now that the barriers were down, they communicated well, in and out of the bedroom.

With his mind made up, he didn't want to waste time. He didn't want to risk her pulling a disappearing act on him like she had her half brother. Not that Ella had any reason to flee. The way she'd clung to him last night in his bed he was certain she'd be more than open to his proposition. A union—a marriage—that would suit them both.

When he hit the sidewalk and his gaze landed on the car, his pace slowed then came to a dead stop. Near the passenger side window stood a man—medium height, swarthy complexion. Tristan had the feeling he wasn't asking directions.

All senses swinging to red alert, Tristan picked up his pace, but by the time he reached the car, the stranger had seen him and slid around the corner. Tristan ached to follow, but seeing Ella staring straight ahead, looking dazed, he jumped into the driver's side instead. He placed the bag containing the gifts in the door pocket, then frowning, reached for her hand. It was icy.

"Who was that?"

She looked blankly at him at first, then awareness broke through the daze. "It was him. Scarpini. He followed us."

Tristan belted his fist against the steering wheel and swore. He jammed his key into the ignition. "We're going to the police."

"No!"

The same trepidation he'd seen the other night when he'd mentioned the law widened her eyes now. He wanted to empathize: she didn't want to churn up bad memories of being questioned after her mother's death. But, dammit, he couldn't let this slide.

"Then *I'll* talk to him," Tristan offered. How dare that man phone his house, follow his car, harass the woman he planned to marry?

Ella's complexion dropped another shade. "There's no need for you to get involved."

"There's every reason."

She gripped his hand. "If I stick to my guns, he has to give up eventually."

Tristan growled and, after a tense, prolonged moment, reluctantly nodded. "But if that bastard bothers you again, I won't be thinking—I'll be acting."

Her lips trembled on a grateful smile, then she let

out a breath. "We should probably get going or we'll be more than fashionably late."

When they pulled up outside of Josh's two-story Mediterranean-style home a short time after, Tristan's insides jerked. The new silver Porsche in the drive was Cade's.

He exhaled heavily. And the day had started out so well.

They walked in together, Ella's arm linked securely through his. There were perhaps thirty people dotted around the perimeter of the architect-designed pool, which faced a spectacular view of colorful yachts drifting over the harbor below.

Head and shoulders above the rest of the guests stood Cade, mirror aviator glasses hiding his haunting yellow eyes—their father's eyes.

Tristan's free hand clenched at his side at the same time Josh appeared, partly breaking the tension.

"Hey, big bother." After the customary bear hug, Josh held out his hand to Ella. "I'm Josh Barkley."

Returning the smile, Ella accepted his hand. "Ella Jacob. We've spoken on the phone."

Josh's frown was amused. "We have?"

Before Tristan could explain, Josh's fiancée, Grace, left off speaking with a middle-aged couple—her parents, Tristan presumed from the resemblance—and flung her arms around him. Tristan chuckled. Petite, blond, from a respected, well-to-do family and always with the friendliest of smiles—she was perfect for Josh. He wished them nothing but happiness.

Grace pulled away. "Thank you so much for coming,

Tristan. It means so much to us both." She held out her hand to Ella. "I don't believe we've met."

After Ella introduced herself again, Grace linked her arm through Josh's and looked between the two of them. "So, have you been seeing each other long?"

Tristan grinned. Straight to the point. He liked that. "Ella works for me."

Josh beamed. "Oh, you're *that* Ella. I've heard all about your talents in the kitchen. I could kick myself for not getting around to inviting myself over and enjoying them myself." He gazed adoringly at Grace. "Been busy with other things."

Grace's matching smile drifted to Tristan. "I think it's easy to see that Ella's much more than Tristan's housekeeper now."

While Ella blushed, Tristan linked his arm around her waist. Grace was definitely on the right track. And if everything went according to his plan, his and Ella's engagement announcement would come next.

Grace snuggled into Josh's arm. "Josh and I have been dating for three months." She dropped her voice. "If my folks are a little frosty today it's because they'd like us to wait. But we both know it's forever."

Josh smiled. "When you know, you know."

Tristan was aware that Grace's family fortune was equal to the Barkley brothers' coffers. She wasn't after Josh for prestige or security—just as Ella wasn't after his. Tristan wasn't forgetting that Ella would marry a plumber as soon as a CEO, the defining factor being love.

He had no problem with love, per se. Love would grow, but only after the most important pieces of a relationship were in place—trust, respect, friendship. The kind of common-sense, solid love his parents had never shared.

Grace took Ella's hand. "These two boys don't see each other half as often as they should. Why don't we leave them to catch up while you meet my family?"

Ella asked Tristan, "Is that all right?"

When Tristan saw Cade sauntering over, he understood that Grace was clearing the path to get any initial brotherly discord out of the way.

He nodded. "Go ahead."

As Ella and Grace moved off, Cade reached the men and put out his hand. For Josh's sake, Tristan gritted his teeth and accepted the gesture.

Cade removed his sunglasses. "Pleasant day for it."

Rather than look at his eyes, Tristan inspected the clear blue sky. "Yep."

"Apologies for intruding on your privacy the other night," Cade added.

"Don't mention it."

"I hope it didn't take too long for you to cool down after I left."

"Please don't concern yourself."

Cade's wry smile said he saw through the sarcasm. He slanted his head. "Don't suppose you've thought anymore about my offer?"

When Tristan took a breath, Josh must have anticipated the shrapnel about to fly and interrupted. "Why don't you guys come over and meet the rest of the guests?"

Tristan held his hand up at Josh.

"I'd like to answer this first." He served Cade an ice-cold look. "Like I told you the other night, there's nothing to think about. Nothing to discuss—now, later, here or anywhere else."

Pushing his hands into his dark trouser pockets, Cade muttered, "Still as stubborn as ever."

A growl rumbled in Tristan's chest. "And you're still as big a pain in the—"

"Hey!" Josh stepped in to physically separate the rivals. "Fellas, keep it nice."

After a tense moment, Cade tipped his head while Tristan scrubbed his jaw and grudgingly nodded once, too.

Josh was so much like their mother—fair hair, striking blue eyes, the mediator—while Cade was the epitome of their father.

A self-serving bastard.

Bristling, Tristan spun on his heel. He needed some space before he did something he might regret. He'd meet Josh's guests later.

Josh followed him to a quiet lawn around the side of the house.

One hand on his hip, the other cradling his hot forehead, Tristan glared at the ground. "He makes me want to kick something. *Hard.*"

"You two haven't changed." Josh walked past Tristan to collect a baseball off a far ledge and roll it from hand to hand. "Always competing."

Josh threw the ball. Almost, but not quite, taken off guard, Tristan caught it and grinned. Josh knew pitching a baseball had always been Tristan's premium way to let off steam.

Tristan concentrated on his target then shot the ball back. "Competition's a good thing," he pointed out.

Rigging Barkley's board decisions and sleeping with your brother's girlfriend were not.

They tossed the ball to and fro a few times before Josh asked, "I know you get hives whenever it's mentioned but, seriously, why don't you consider going back to Barkley's? Think about it. If you two could get over your rift, our hotels could expand to be world leaders."

Tristan smirked. Nice try. "Why not you and Cade?"

"Uncompromising success takes two hundred per-cent commitment. I want a life."

"And I don't?"

"Hasn't been evident lately." Grinning, Josh tossed the ball back hard. "Although you might have turned a corner now you've hooked up with Ella."

About to throw again, Tristan heard Cade's laugh, followed by a woman's. Josh had to duck when the ball left Tristan's hand and the wild missile almost took off his head.

Not waiting for Josh—no time—Tristan charged away. Cade was talking with Ella—only Ella—in a foliaged corner near the pool.

Tristan stopped before them. "Funny joke?" he asked, with not a drop of humour in his voice.

Ella sized up his expression and immediately so-bered. "Your brother was just telling me about—"

"What?" Tristan growled at Cade. "What were you telling her about?"

Cade looked perplexed. *What an actor.* "We were talking about you."

He could just imagine.

Ella touched Tristan's arm. "Would you like some-thing to eat? There's a beautiful spread."

"I'm not hungry," he ground out. "In fact, we need to go."

Cade bringing up Barkley Hotels again, then Josh, now this. Coming here had been a mistake. And it could only get worse. For Tristan, happy families time was over.

Lobbing an apology Josh and Grace's way, Tristan took Ella's arm. He strode off, Ella half a step behind.

At the car, he thumbed the automatic release on his key control and opened her door. When he slid in the driver's side and, still overheated, wrung the steering wheel with both hands, Ella spoke up.

"I know today was difficult, but you don't need to be upset about Cade and me talking. I was telling him how happy I've been working for you."

He slid her a look. "And that's why you were both laughing?"

Her brow furrowed. "He was telling me if anyone needs a cook, it's you. He said when you were seven, you once made your ice cream with chunks of cooking chocolate, a liter of milk and a can of whipped cream. You were so proud he didn't have the heart to turn down seconds when you offered."

A sweet story. Might even tug some heartstrings, but Tristan held himself firm. "A lot of water's passed under the bridge since then."

And he wasn't about to forgive and forget. Cade could keep his filthy mitts off Ella. The SOB would take her just to prove he could.

Tristan fired the engine and shoved the stick in Reverse.

"Are we going home?" she asked.

He thought for a moment then he threw his arm over the passenger backrest and, looking behind, reversed the car in a swift but precise arc onto the road. He planted his foot and the car sped off.

"I'd like to take you to a place I think you'd be interested in seeing." Somewhere that would get his sights back on the bull's eye.

They barely spoke during the thirty-minute drive. Not because Tristan was trying to be difficult…he simply needed time to shake off the prickling sensation left from his older brother's poisonous presence. When they parked on a vast and magnificent stretch of land by the sea, Tristan had regained a measure of his composure.

They got out of the car and Tristan inhaled the fresh, briny air. The rolling emerald waves always revitalized him; this particular quiet corner of the world seemed to hold a special kind of magic.

In a pretty blue-cotton dress and white sandals, Ella held her hair, which waved in golden ribbons around her head in the stiff breeze. "Tristan, this is *amazing*."

They strolled toward the ocean. "All I need is the go-ahead from Rufus and people from all over the world can come here to enjoy five-star comfort and a mega-star view."

He'd double his fortune. Who the hell needed Barkley Hotels?

She sighed. "Imagine living here. It'd be like living in paradise."

"A couple of years from now, anyone with an obscene holiday budget can find out."

She let go her hair and hugged herself against the cool wind. "You really need to do it, don't you?"

His gaze quizzed hers. "Of course I need to do it. I've spent a bucket load of money, I can't count how many hours—"

"I mean, show your brother you can be more successful than he is."

His stomach kicked. He shoved his hands into his pockets and looked back at the sea. "That's part of it."

They both focused on the crashing waves for a long moment before she murmured, "I know what you told me about Cade…"

He examined her hesitant expression and frowned. "Please don't say you don't believe me."

Her face filled with sympathy. "It's just…after meeting him today it's hard to grasp…how he could do something so abhorrent as seduce his brother's girlfriend. I couldn't help thinking how much he reminds me of you."

Tristan's lip curled. "People aren't always what they seem."

Even brothers. She might be naive in a lot of ways, but shouldn't Ella know that wolves grin just before they bite? Hadn't her half brother charmed her mother while trying his best to have her change her will?

They turned back and when they reached the car, he asked, "Can you wait here a moment?"

Her brows fell together but she nodded. He rounded the hood and opened his door. When he returned to the front of the car, he presented her with the packet.

She looked inside, saw the packaging and her face lit up. "A birthday gift?"

"Hope you like it."

Carefully she unwrapped the paper and ribbon and

sighed when she saw the gift. "A gold pen. It's so shiny."

He scratched the top of his ear. "It's to autograph that bestselling book you're going to write."

Her gaze jumped up and now she truly was smiling. "My cookbook?"

He nodded.

Her cool hand touched his cheek as she kissed his lips lightly. "That's so thoughtful. Thank you."

Drawn by her sparkling blue eyes, he fought the urge to go fetch the earrings. But he'd already decided to delay presenting her with that more personal gift until after he'd received her response to his question. *The* question.

He held her hand and gave it a meaningful squeeze. "I had an incredible time last night."

Her eyes shone with heartfelt understanding. "I'd think it was all a dream if we weren't standing here now."

"Ella, you're different from any woman I've known."

She laughed. "You mean the supermodels or the society princesses?"

He gave a crooked grin. "My point exactly. You're wholesome and uncomplicated."

Her left eyebrow shot up at a wry angle. "You must have forgotten my half brother, the stalker."

A muscle in his jaw flexed. "I'm not forgetting him. In fact, your situation with that excuse of a man gives my proposition even more weight."

Her head slanted. "Your proposition?"

"We're compatible, you and I."

Her warm smile told him she was remembering last night and this morning. "You could say that."

"I respect you, Ella."

Her gaze grew more questioning. "I respect you, too."

"Aside from that," he grinned, "you do amazing things for my libido."

Her cheeks pinked up. "You'll swell my head."

"Enough to say yes?"

"Yes to what?

He filled his lungs and searched her eyes. "Ella, I want to marry you."

Eight

The sound of waves crashing faded beneath the sudden rush of blood in Ella's ears. The world was spinning, setting her completely off balance. She had to focus on Tristan's smiling eyes or risk toppling over.

"I'm sorry?" she croaked out. "Did I hear you right?"

Curling her arm around his, he lifted and kissed her hand. "I want to marry you. I want you to be my bride."

Her words came out a hoarse, disbelieving whisper. "Now I know I'm dreaming."

"Think about it. We'd be perfect together. You're everything I want in a wife. When you're with me, it feels…" His shoulders rolled back. "The only word is *right*. That feeling's been knocking at the back of my brain these whole eight months. This last week—last night—simply put it into sharp focus."

She coughed out a laugh. "At the risk of sounding clichéd, this is all so sudden."

He chuckled. "It is, but I wanted to put this to you sooner rather than later. I didn't want any chance of you up and leaving before I'd told you how I felt."

Yesterday she'd believed it was too soon to think about love. Yet today—now—every overjoyed fiber of her being was shooting her closer to that conclusion. Her growing feelings for Tristan had been a wonderful work in progress. She wondered if Tristan was saying that he was falling in love with her, too.

She smiled into his eyes. "How *do* you feel, Tristan?"

"Certain," he declared. "Convinced that we'd make an ideal pair. You won't want for a thing. Of course, we'll need to hire another housekeeper, not a live-in this time." His thumb brushed the sensitive inside of her wrist. "We'll want our privacy."

Ideal pair? Not want for a thing? She waited, hopeful, knowing there must be more. "And?"

His brow pinched. "Well, I wouldn't expect you to cook all the time, only if you wanted to. You'll be accompanying me to business and social events. I don't mind if we have a big or a small wedding. I'm thinking with your temperament you'd go for small." He thought for a moment. "What else would you like to know?"

The air seeped from her lungs. With each word the foundation of what he was suggesting became clearer. She pressed the pen set against her stomach as her insides clutched. "You're talking about an *arrangement?*"

Relief at her understanding shone in his eyes. "Precisely. An arrangement that would suit us both."

So, this proposal was for a marriage of convenience. The term sounded archaic, so businesslike, and yet Ella knew in her heart that her assumption wasn't mistaken. After feeling elated, now she merely felt numb.

The happiness she saw in his eyes had nothing to do with love. He'd had a run of ambitious women who, he believed, had coveted him for his money as much as anything. Now he thought *she* would make the perfect accessory. Wholesome, uncomplaining, anything-else-I-can-get-for-you Ella.

This was so far from the kind of proposal she'd expected from the man of her dreams. Remarkably, it seemed she was the woman of Tristan's dreams—but in a practical rather than emotional sense.

A thought surfaced and lit a spark of hope.

If she accepted his proposal—if they did become man and wife—was it possible he might grow to love her? she wondered. Was that too much for a lowly housekeeper to hope for?

She bit the inside of her cheek to stem the emotion building at the back of her eyes. "Can I think it over?"

He flicked a glance back at the car but then smiled. "It's an important decision. You *should* think it over." He stepped closer and set their clasped hands against his hard, hot chest. "Here's something to help you make up your mind."

His mouth touched hers in the perfect persuasive kiss. Almost persuasive enough to make her forget that at this point he was after a collaboration, not a soulmate.

Two weeks later, Ella still hadn't given Tristan an answer. They'd continued to share a bed and she'd continued to be his housekeeper. Tristan was delighted with the first arrangement and not so pleased by the second, though he didn't openly object to her continuing to dust and iron. He was giving her time to think his proposition through without any pressure, just as he'd said he would. And given she hadn't agreed to his proposal of marriage yet, she couldn't very well give up her duties.

However, news she'd received today had as good as made up her mind. She'd been stunned at first, but as the shock had worn off, she only hoped that Tristan would be as thrilled as she was.

She was pregnant. Having Tristan's baby. Whenever she imagined the precious seed growing inside her, she could barely contain her awe and excitement.

Still, she needed to keep the startling fact that they were going to be parents to herself a few hours longer. Tonight Mayor Rufus was coming to dinner. She didn't want Tristan distracted from what must be the most important business meeting of his career to date.

If Rufus gave the nod on the land rezoning, Tristan could go ahead with construction of his dream project. This deal wasn't about money, it was about self-worth. He needed this so he could move forever from beneath the shadow of big brother Cade.

Ella added the final seasoning to the chowder, remembering the scrumptious hours she'd spent in his bed. Tristan could be a shoe salesman and it wouldn't matter a fig to her.

When the kitchen extension rang, her heart leapt to her throat as it had every time the phone had peeled these past weeks. But she was overreacting. She hadn't heard from Drago Scarpini since that day by Tristan's car. Perhaps knowing she and Tristan were more than employee and employer had given him pause for thought. One look at Tristan's determined bearing confirmed he wasn't a man to mess with.

Wiping her hand down her apron, she picked up the receiver. "Barkley residence."

"Eleanor. You sound as charming as ever."

As her legs lost strength, she sank into the seat behind her. "It's you."

Scarpini only laughed. Gulping down a breath, she regained her composure. "You're wasting your time."

"On the contrary. I've invested too much time in this to give up now."

She wanted to fling the phone at the wall. Instead she kept her voice steady. "Tristan and I will go to the police."

"Oooh, Tristan and I," he sing-songed. "This does sound serious. Should I expect a wedding invitation in the near future?"

"That is none of your business."

He laughed again, genuinely amused this time. "So you've struck gold! Congratulations. I'm sure your wealthy lover won't miss the little recompense you throw my way."

"You don't frighten me. Nothing you say or do will convince me to give you a penny more."

"I'd rethink that. Tristan Barkley's a mighty fine catch. You wouldn't want to risk losing him."

She thought of the police that night, their wary, almost accusing looks, but she swallowed her fear.

Her chin kicked up. "I have nothing to be ashamed of."

His voice lowered to a deadly growl. "If you want to push me, be warned, I'll only push harder." His voice lightened. "I see the Barkley property gates are open. Seems like an ideal time to pay your fiancé a visit."

When the phone disconnected in her ear, Ella let her head fall between her legs as nausea pushed up in her throat and perspiration broke on her brow. Scarpini was obviously within walking distance of the house. The last thing she'd wanted was to bother Tristan with anything tonight, but she had no choice. Scarpini sounded deranged enough to do as he threatened and knock on the front door. What he intended to say, she couldn't guess. But Tristan needed to be forewarned.

Two minutes later, standing in the doorway of his bedroom—their bedroom—Ella pressed down a shaky breath and uttered the words.

"I need to talk to you."

Looking scrumptious in dark trousers and a crisp white shirt, Tristan finished securing a gold cufflink, checked his wristwatch then moved away from his mirrored wardrobe toward her. "Does this have to do with tonight's dinner? Are you missing some ingredient?"

If only it were that simple.

She shook her head. "Everything's prepared."

Her face must have been white. He cupped her shoulders and his frown deepened. "My God, you're shaking."

She opened her mouth, ready to blurt it all out, but the doorbell rang and every muscle in her body tensed.

Tristan's attention shifted and his hands dropped to his sides. "The mayor's early."

"It's not the mayor," she shot out. "Scarpini phoned. He said he's paying us a visit."

Tristan's expression clouded over until it resembled a thunderstorm. "He *what?*"

"I have no idea what he expects to happen when he gets here."

Tristan threw back his shoulders and strode out of the room ahead of her. "I've had all I'm prepared to take from that—"

His curses trailed behind him as Ella followed. Downstairs, when Tristan swung open the front door, she straightened, ready to face whatever might come. But Scarpini didn't stand on their doorstep. It was Mayor Rufus after all.

"George." Tristan ran a hand through his hair, looked past the mayor's shoulder then offered his hand to his guest. "Good to see you."

Accepting the gesture, the mayor's smile grew when he saw Ella.

Ella swayed on her feet, giddy with relief. If she and Scarpini had to have a showdown, she hoped it wouldn't be tonight. This dinner was too important to Tristan.

Somehow she willed her rubbery mouth to work. "Hello, Mayor."

He presented a labeled bottle. "I've been looking forward to this evening."

She reflexively accepted the wine. "I hope you're not disappointed."

The mayor flicked Tristan a glance. "I'm sure it'll be a memorable occasion for everyone."

Tristan's gaze scanned the shadowed front lawn before he shut the door.

The mayor frowned. "Are you expecting another guest?"

"There'd been talk of it, but I'm sure that's all it was. Talk." He gestured the mayor inside. "Would you care for a drink before dinner?"

Looking a little uncertain, the mayor nodded. "A whisky sour, thank you."

"Ella, we'll continue our conversation later."

While Tristan showed the mayor to the dining room, Ella dragged her leaden feet to the kitchen. Barely aware of her actions, she garnished the clam chowder.

When she delivered the first course, the mayor inhaled and patted his chest. "That smells delicious." She set the plate before him and he chuckled. "How did you know chowder was my favorite?" He quizzed Tristan. "Did you tell her?"

Tristan nodded. "I thought you'd enjoy it."

The mayor explained to Ella, "My wife passed away not long before our daughter—" His lips pressed together and he lowered his eyes. "Well, thing is my wife was happiest when she was in the kitchen."

Ella joined the dots. The mayor's wife had died not long before Bindy.

For a moment Ella forget her own dilemma. It was terrible to lose someone close. It must have been horrible to lose two people you loved within a short span of time.

She wanted to say something supportive. "Sounds as if your wife took great care of you."

The mayor's eyes grew distant before he looked at her more closely and smiled. "Good women aren't so easy to find."

When the men returned to their conversation, Ella slipped back to the kitchen. With her mind flitting between Scarpini's antics and the baby growing inside of her, she garnished the main course. In the dining room again, she retrieved the empty bowls, pleased with the mayor's compliments. When she returned with their meals, he and Tristan were discussing the land rezoning.

The mayor sipped his wine. "I don't see a problem, Tristan, but with one condition." He set his glass down. "The council would like you to donate a portion of the land to develop a harbor for a marina. You won't need to worry about management issues. We'll have someone look after that. But you will need to work together on the development and coordinating ongoing logistics."

Tristan sat back and rapped his knuckles on the table. "I have very specific objectives, George. After dessert I'll take you into the study and show you the plans—"

"I've already gone through them with the town planner in great detail. They're innovative, well thought-out and bound to afford you a successful enterprise."

The mayor leaned forward as Ella moved around his chair to pepper Tristan's meal.

"I've thought long and hard about this compromise," the mayor continued. "I'm happy with the rezoning as long as you'll cooperate with this marina. It'll mean increased employment opportunities and prestige for the area. The voters are eager to advance the community."

Tristan rubbed the back of his neck, his smile apologetic. "I've thought this through carefully, too. My investors are expecting a certain return and what you propose will cut into that profit."

While Ella topped off the wine glasses, the mayor's face reddened. "Son, the marina *will* bring money in."

"Not enough to compensate for the added headaches."

The mayor's hand fisted on the tablecloth. "What you're saying is you're not prepared to bring in anyone else. Not prepared to consider anybody else's…"

Ella left the room and that conversation behind. She could think only of her stomach—a churning mass of nerves.

Would Scarpini show up? How would Tristan react when he found out he was going to be a dad?

Her mind half on the job, she opened the oven door. As she pulled out the pie dish, the phone's ring pealed through the room. Startled out of her skin, she dropped the dish and the noise of smashing glass exploded like a bomb blast through the high ceilings. A lick of hot caramel splashed her bare legs. She cried out in pain, and then bit her lip against the tears about to spill. What on earth else could happen today? she wondered in panic.

"What's going on here?"

Her breathing ragged, she tried to focus through the moisture edging her eyes. Tristan stood at the kitchen entrance, his face dark, his body poised for action.

She scrubbed the shaky heel of her hand across her wet cheek. "I dropped the pie dish."

He moved forward and held her shoulders as he searched her eyes. "Was that him? Did Scarpini call again?"

She couldn't look at him. "I've ruined dessert."

His grip tightened as his voice dropped to an urgent growl. "Ella, tell me."

She peered into his stormy, expectant eyes—eyes that said, I'm here… I can help.

She swallowed against the swelling ache in her throat and told him.

"I'm having a baby."

Time stood still before his jaw unhinged. Then he dropped his hold as if he too had been burned.

Ella covered her mouth. That thought had been pushing at the forefront of her mind for hours, but how could she have blurted it out now, at the worst possible time?

After a strained moment, color returned to Tristan's face. He kept his voice low. "We've been sleeping together two weeks. Is it possible?"

She struggled to order her thoughts and explain. "I needed a script for my hypertension medication."

He followed her thread. "High blood pressure…it runs in your family."

She nodded. "Today, during the check-up, my doctor asked the usual questions. I mentioned I was a couple of days late. We did a test." She swallowed again. "They're very accurate these days."

Tristan's frame tilted. His hip hit the counter as he dragged a hand down his face. "We're…*pregnant?*"

The mayor's disapproving voice broke the moment. "Congratulations."

Tristan swung around.

The mayor lifted a gray-tuft eyebrow. "I came to see if I could help. It sounded as if someone was being attacked."

"Nothing that drastic," Tristan groaned. "But it might be best to cut our evening short. I'm sorry."

"By the sound of it, you shouldn't be apologizing to me." The mayor nodded at Ella. "Good luck, my dear." His tone said she'd need it. "I'll let myself out."

When the mayor had left, Tristan faced her again.

Ella's midsection twisted. "He didn't look too happy."

"Don't worry about George. I'll work that out later. Right now you and I have something more important to discuss."

She took heart that he thought her news was more important than his pet project, but then she flinched. "Are you upset?"

"I'm surprised." The line between his brows disappeared. "But, no, I'm not upset. And I think this situation answers the question I asked two weeks ago. We'll get married as soon as possible. If I'm going to be a father, I want to make certain the child bears my name. No mistake."

A wave of relief washed over her. Her own father had been a wonderful influence in her life. Ideally, Ella wanted this child to grow up in a traditional household, which included two parents. Already she could imagine her baby's smile. She hadn't planned to conceive, but now that she had, she well understood how powerful maternal instinct could be.

The phone rang again. Ella jumped but before she could speak, Tristan strode to the extension and snatched up the receiver.

"Who is this?" He nodded and growled. "This is the last time you contact anyone to do with this house, do you hear me? You try this kind of stunt again and I'll see you in jail."

He slammed the phone down and strode back to Ella.

"I'll have a police friend from the neighborhood station track Scarpini down and pay him a visit to explain the situation—back off or face charges. I was ready to break that jerk's jaw before your news tonight. No way in the world is he getting near you now."

She opened her mouth, but he held up a hand.

"No reprieves this time. After I speak with my friend, I'll organize the paperwork and we'll fly to New Zealand for the wedding."

"You want to get married overseas?"

"New Zealand requires only three working days' lead time for Intention to Marry applications."

He *was* in a hurry. "In Australia you only need a month."

She knew because at one point she'd considered marrying Sean. What a mistake.

"I want to marry you and I want to do it as soon as possible." He took and squeezed her hands so tightly his grip almost hurt. "Ella, is there anything else you need to tell me?"

"I'd have thought you'd heard enough."

He didn't smile at her joke. "So there's nothing?"

She shook her head, wanting to ask the same of him. Was there anything he'd like to tell her? Perhaps that he was starting to see their relationship as something more than a mutually beneficial contract. That, after the wondrous nights they'd spent together, his feelings for her had grown. If they did in fact marry, would she ever hear the words her father had said to her mother every morning and every night?

I love you.

But while his expression eased, the words she longed to hear didn't come.

"Then Monday you should shop for a wedding gown," he said instead. "This time next week, you'll be Mrs. Tristan Barkley."

Nine

"You may now kiss the bride."

Hearing the minister's request, Ella clung to her lily bouquet and tried to convince herself this wedding—*her* wedding—was really happening. Smiling into her eyes, Tristan trailed two fingers around her cheek and lifted her chin until his mouth met hers.

His kiss was lasting and meaningful, an embrace that released ripples of joy through her bloodstream and filled her with the promise of what the coming years would bring. This morning they'd flown to New Zealand. As of this minute they were man and wife.

But it would take more than a consummation of their marriage contract to cement a true bond. Full commitment would happen when the light that had shone in his eyes just now transformed into words. Words of love she ached to hear and offer in return.

Tristan relinquished his hold and gently broke away at the same time the delighted minister cast back his cloaked shoulders and closed his book. "Now we only need to get some papers signed."

Tristan kept his smiling eyes on Ella. "And then it's done."

After the newlyweds had signed, a lovely couple who were staying at the mountain resort where Tristan had booked the honeymoon suite witnessed the document. With the minister's good wishes, Ella and Tristan left the reception lounge through a set of expansive, floor-to-ceiling doors, which lured them out to appreciate the spectacular view.

On the chilly balcony, Tristan stood behind her, drawing her back against his solid warmth and circling her waist with his arms as they gazed out over the soaring mountain peaks spotted with snow. The clean air was filled with a blend of spring bouquets, as well as laughter from a group of tourists wandering up the chateau's shrub-lined path.

Sighing, she leaned her head back against his chest. "I've never seen anything more beautiful."

He kissed her crown. "I have."

He turned her around so they faced each other. His hands laced together low on her back, he touched his forehead to hers. "Are you disappointed we didn't have a traditional wedding?"

Once she'd envisaged her wedding with a church full of people, mountains of flowers, her mother patting away a tear, her father proud and standing beside her…

Setting aside any regret, she answered truthfully. "I wouldn't swap today for anything."

He kissed her and she melted against him as the delicious heat in her belly spread lower. She was nearly breathless when their lips parted.

Grinning, he nipped her bottom lip. "I've organized a private dinner. I think we should go and enjoy the view from our room."

Her skin flashed hot at the thought of being alone with Tristan—his sexy smile, his sexier body. Her fingers kneaded his shirt. "I think so, too."

They hadn't made love since she'd told him about the pregnancy. Oh, she'd slept in his bed, and he'd held her close each night. There'd been no mistaking his state of physical arousal, but he hadn't gone beyond kissing, although she'd ached for him to.

He hadn't explained why he'd refrained. Perhaps he was coming to terms with the idea of becoming a married man. Maybe he wanted to keep their wedding night special, as if it wouldn't be anyway. Whatever his reason, in the dark when he'd held her she'd sensed his mind ticking over.

As they traveled up in the lift, she gazed down at the gold wedding band on her finger and, next to it, the dazzling tear-shaped diamond that effused a rainbow of prisms.

He'd proposed on the basis that they were compatible, that a marriage arrangement would work well for them both. Did he hope that his love for her would follow? She couldn't believe that a passionate man like Tristan would purposely—coldly—preclude love from the marriage equation, particularly now that there would be a baby. She had only to think of their child, the newborn she would hold in her arms one day soon, and her heart overflowed. Surely Tristan felt the same way.

When they reached their door, he swiped the card then swept her up into his arms. As her feet left the ground, the air whooshed from her lungs in a delighted rush.

Grinning, he kicked the door open and crossed the threshold. He didn't set her down until they reached the center of the room, where a table was laden with an exquisite array of fruits, breads, savory dishes and a silver-plated ice bucket chilling a bottle of champagne.

The ice crunched as he retrieved the bottle. A moment later, the pop of its cork reverberated through the room and foam frothed over his hand.

She laughed and he dropped a cloth over the bottle to stem the flow.

"Glasses!" Laughing too, he waved his free hand at the flutes. "Hurry!"

She grabbed the glasses and he poured.

When he set down the bottle, he raised his glass. "To us."

Suddenly overwhelmed by the significance of the moment, she raised her glass too and murmured, "To us."

As they sipped, she noticed a fire lit and crackling behind them. Despite the dropping temperature outside, the room was toasty and threaded with the subtle scent of rising heat and glowing wood.

He slid his glass onto the table. "I have an idea." He crossed to the bed and swept the gold brocade quilt off the mattress and onto the carpet before the fire. "Let's have a picnic."

She drifted over. "Mmm, very romantic."

"But I'm not sure we're dressed for the occasion."

Stepping closer, she ran a fingertip down his blue silk tie. "Maybe we should go change."

His smile was wicked. "There's no need to go anywhere."

He looped his arms around her and, keeping his eyes on hers, slowly unzipped her dress. "I'll say it again. You look beautiful in this gown, but after almost a week without you, you'll look even more beautiful out of it."

The dress dropped. Her cheeks glowing, she stepped out of the ripples of exquisite imported white silk.

He let out a long, low whistle at her new lacy lingerie. "That's *perfect* attire for an indoor picnic," he said. "I think we should kick off our feast with strawberries." He tipped his chin. "They're there on the table."

Falling back into her housekeeper role, she immediately crossed to fetch the fruit. When she returned, his head was slanted, his gaze feeding on each step of her advance.

Shifting his weight to one leg, he crossed his arms and grinned. "Have I mentioned how much I like your lingerie?"

Grinning back, she lowered the plate onto the quilt and then set her hands on her hips. Not so long ago she would have died of embarrassment to stand before him like this. Now she felt proud of the way his eyes danced.

"Would you like me to get anything else?" she teased.

He ripped off his tie and dropped it. "Suddenly I'm not hungry."

Grabbing her wrist, he brought her near. With his hands cupping her waist, he dropped his head to savor the slope of her neck.

She shivered with undiluted longing. "You know, we didn't have much lunch," she teased again. "Maybe we should eat first."

He flicked open the strapless bra clasp at her back. "We'll eat *after.*"

As his mouth closed over hers, her hands drifted up, impatiently undoing his buttons then dragging the shirt-tails from his trousers. He maneuvered her bra from between them and groaned against her parted, desperate lips, "Lie down."

Happy to oblige, she sank onto the quilt. Her eyes remained glued on his actions as he speedily stripped off his clothes then stood before her gloriously naked— every muscle pumped, hard and gleaming in the flickering firelight.

He joined her, his powerful chest hovering near, his forearms resting near either side of her head. But instead of taking her mouth, his lips trailed her throat toward her cleavage. When the hot tip of his tongue traveled over and around one nipple, rhythmically flicking the bead, she could've gone up in flames. His erection ground against her as his teeth grazed, tugging the sensitive peak until, half out of her mind, she moaned for him to stop.

He did. But only to roll onto his back and swing her

above him. When she straddled his hips, he snatched her panties' crotch aside then maneuvered her forward and back until she felt him throb and slide inside.

Filled with him, her movements stilled.

In awe, she watched the shadows flicker over his face.

Then slowly she began to move above him, his hands on her hips guiding her strokes, increasing her rhythm until all her concentration compressed in on the sizzling hub pulsing inside of her. As his fingers fanned over her abdomen, the pad of his thumb angled down between her legs and there he gently rubbed.

A bone-melting moment later, an inferno imploded then flashed electrifying white heat through her system. As his body locked then shuddered beneath her, her contractions kept coming until finally the flurry of sparks began to shower back down.

She fell on top of him, exhausted, exhilarated.

And in the shimmering afterglow of their lovemaking, when he held her close but didn't say the words, she didn't despair. They had time enough. Time for his love to grow.

They ate strawberries, some bread and dip and then they made love again, with less urgency this time, knowing they had tomorrow—times ten thousand.

They ate more and later lay in bed, under the covers. Ella curled up around his hard body and traced circles through the crisp hair on his chest. Her fingertip slid up to the hot, beating hollow of his throat and higher, over his raspy chin, then across the soft contrast of his perfect lips.

She felt safer than she ever had. Not least of all because Tristan had kept his word.

Last Monday he'd filed a complaint with his police friend who had located and dropped in on Drago Scarpini. Surely that would be the end of it. Unfortunately, Tristan hadn't yet been able to rectify the damage done to his negotiations with the mayor. George Rufus had been officially unavailable since last Saturday night.

Remembering that Tristan had checked his messages earlier, she pushed up slightly and rested her chin on her stacked fist on his chest. "Did the mayor return your call yesterday?"

Tristan's jaw shifted. "No."

"What will you do next?"

"Sit on it for now."

In other words, try to find a way to have his resort without giving up on his vision of it. If she hadn't dropped that dish—if she'd served up that dessert instead of smashing it all over the floor and announcing her pregnancy—perhaps Tristan would have had time enough to talk the mayor around to his way of thinking.

"Do you think you'll need to give in to his request for land for a marina now?"

His chest inflated and he shifted to cradle the back of his head in his hands. "Where there's a will, there's a way. There's a solution to the problem." In the fire's dying shadows, she saw his eyes narrow. "I just need to find it." He frowned down his nose at her. "But why are we talking about Mayor Rufus?" He craned slightly to kiss her brow. "Let's talk about what comes next for us. Let's talk about you and me."

She rolled onto her side and propped her head in her hand as excitement spiraled through her. "I'm all ears."

He scooped hair behind her ear, the way he did whenever he was thinking deeply about her. "We're going to have a big family, you and I. Seven children. Four sons and three daughters."

She stopped to quiz his eyes. "Are you serious?"

"Josh and I used to say we each wanted enough for a baseball team." He winked at her. "Want to learn how to pitch?"

She laughed a little nervously. "But, Tristan, *seven?*"

"What? It's a lucky number."

She chewed her lip. "If you really mean it, there's got to be a better reason than lucky numbers and baseball teams."

His smile faded. A muscle in his jaw flexed before he stared up at the ceiling and explained, "Our father didn't have much time for us. In fact, we rarely saw him. Josh and I used to goof around on the baseball diamond in the park, pretending we were dads coaching and cheering on our kids. The idea grew from there and just stuck."

She took in his deeper rationale then asked quietly, "Cade didn't join in the discussion on families?"

Tristan's mouth thinned. "Cade's so self-absorbed, I doubt he'd have even one. Unless it was a mistake."

Her stomach dropped and she pushed up on her elbow. "Like ours was a mistake?"

He brought her back down so they lay on their sides, facing each other. "*This*, my darling, was meant to be, just as the minister said, from this day forward. In fact, I brought something along, a wedding gift I'd like you to wear on our tenth anniversary and on our *fiftieth.*"

She smiled. Surely those weren't the words of a man who saw marriage merely as a convenience. But before she accepted his gift, she needed to settle their previous conversation.

She eased back into it. "You must see lots of grand-children on our fiftieth."

"Hopefully," he grinned. "Sure." Then his brows tipped together. "Don't you want a big family? I thought you liked looking after home matters. You seemed so excited about the baby."

"I *am* excited. But there's a difference between being someone's housekeeper and running a house-hold that includes seven little lives."

Ella's cousin had had four children before she was twenty-three. She was happy when she wasn't totally exhausted. But Ella had always envisaged having maybe a pigeon pair so she didn't feel as if anyone would miss out on her love and attention.

His concerned face dissolved beneath understand-ing. "I don't expect you to clean the house or look after nine lots of laundry. As soon as we get back I will hire someone to take over your former duties. And when the baby comes, we'll find the best nanny in town."

Ella inwardly cringed. A stranger looking after her baby? Perhaps it was the way of the rich and famous, but she'd come from more grounded stock. "There are lots of things I don't believe parents should leave to a nanny. Like homework and sport days and bath time."

She'd always imagined doing those chores herself, bonding with her children along the way, being in-volved in every facet of their lives…just not seven times over.

"I can help with those things," he offered. "I want to."

That was sweet, she thought. "But you don't get home until late most nights. Young children need their sleep."

His brow lowered and he blinked twice. "What are you saying?"

"Only that producing our own baseball team sounds a little over the top."

His eyes narrowed almost imperceptibly. "How many children do you want? Surely not just one?"

He kept staring at her and the nerves in her stomach pulled tight. "We should have discussed this before…"

"Call me stupid but I assumed…" He frowned. "Seems I assumed wrong."

A light rap on the door broke the moment. Exhaling audibly, Tristan slipped out of bed. "Must be room service to finally collect the trolley."

After pulling on a robe, Tristan answered the door. An exuberant bellboy presented a gift basket. "Flowers and champagne, sir. From Mr. Joshua Barkley."

Tristan tipped the boy and brought the basket inside.

Ella pulled the untucked top sheet off the bed and around her then wandered over to inspect the arrangement. Lilies, orchids, roses… "They're gorgeous."

Tristan read the message. "This is more than a congratulatory card. Josh and Grace have organized a reception for us this weekend."

Ella read the card. It was short notice, but so thoughtful. That was a woman's touch—something she would like to do for a sister if she'd had one. She and Grace were destined to become fast friends.

Scowling, Tristan flapped the card against his thigh. "I won't be happy if Cade dares to show his face."

She threaded one arm around his neck and willed him to see the trust and, yes, love shining from her eyes. Was Cade the outright villain Tristan believed him to be? She simply couldn't believe it. Now that she was his wife, was it her place to say? she wondered.

She came up with a piece of less pointed advice.

"Try not to give anyone that power over you. It'll be our day. Let's just enjoy it regardless of who's there."

"Hell, maybe we should invite Cade over to share a toast."

He was smiling but his eyes were hard as flint.

A little hurt, she let her arm drop. "Maybe we should…if sharing a drink with Cade would help to get you two talking rather than arguing."

A pile of demons haunted Tristan…ghosts who whispered to him about childhood, Barkley Hotels and Bindy Rufus.

With an air of inevitability, he returned the card to its plastic slot in the arrangement. "I think it's time for a little family history to clarify things."

She tilted her head. "If you like."

A pulse beat in his jaw as he stared blankly at the flowers. "Josh was only nine when my mother died, too young to understand what had gone on. But I was thirteen, Cade fifteen. Our mother was an angel and yet our father couldn't resist sleeping with his best friend's wife." His chin tipped up. "She didn't leave a note, but I have no doubt my father's betrayal was the reason she took her life."

Feeling winded, Ella sank down onto the couch

behind her. After a moment, she got her thoughts together. "What does this have to do with Cade?"

His brows shot up. "Isn't it obvious? Like father, like son."

"He was your father, too."

"A man can also make choices."

"And part of those choices include what we choose to believe." He pressed his lips together, annoyed, but she wasn't finished. "Do you truly believe Cade is capable of such a thing?"

A moment of doubt flickered in his eyes before they hardened again. "You don't know my brother."

"Isn't it possible there's another explanation?"

"Sure. Bindy was in the operating theatre and stitched up the wound when Cade had his appendix out?" He set his hands low on his hips. "Why are you so eager to defend him?"

"It's not about defending Cade. It's about finding the truth and giving you peace of mind. You're ready to believe the very worst, but do you have any proof he slept with Bindy other than her word?"

Ella tried to remember what Tristan had said the other week. That Bindy's admission of infidelity had only crystallized what he'd felt more and more—they weren't right for each other. If Bindy had been aware of Tristan distancing himself before that night, she might have said anything to gain his attention. People could say and do some foolish things when they were smashed. Ella had only to remember Sean's behavior to be certain of that. The things he'd said that last night had turned her blood cold. Things like she was too plain and stupid for anyone to love.

"Ella, no one purposely sets out to despise his or her brother. You know that. He brought it on himself."

Or was it more that Cade's guilt made it easier for Tristan to walk away from the pressure of constantly needing to compete with someone who saw him, not as an equal, but rather as a younger brother.

But even if her intuition was right, Tristan wasn't ready to listen.

Rubbing the back of his neck, he turned toward the bathroom. "I'm going to shower."

Ella leaned back against the couch, her mind consumed by thoughts of today's ceremony and the conversation just now, as well as their future. Tristan didn't like to compromise. He liked to win. And he'd won her with so little effort…

She gazed down at her enormous diamond ring, which was a little too big for her finger, then laid that hand on her tummy.

She wondered if Tristan truly saw her as his wife. Or was she merely an employee who'd won a star promotion and the opportunity to produce his heirs?

Ten

Two days later they were back in Sydney. As Tristan stood among friends at the garden-party reception Josh and Grace had organized, he ordered himself to take a deep breath and chill out.

Over the previous two hours, a hundred or so guests had enjoyed a fine selection of finger food, gold label wines and a billion-dollar view, courtesy of the restaurant's vantage point overlooking the harbor, with the giant arch of Sydney Harbour Bridge glittering in the far background.

He'd caught up with friends from business and university. Grace had located some of Ella's friends, too. She was talking and laughing with one now. He sighed looking at his bride. She had no idea how beautiful she was, how she stood out in that simple yet exquisite red dress.

On their wedding day, he'd felt closer to her than ever before. When he'd made love to Ella, knowing his rings had glittered on her finger, he'd found himself considering their union beyond the parameters he'd initially laid out. For the first time since he'd hit on the idea, he'd glimpsed the possibility of their union being something more than simply practical.

But, although a romantic at heart, Ella had gone into the arrangement on the same basis as he had—compatibility, convenience and lastly the fact that they'd conceived. Those were the reasons this marriage made such good sense. And when their talk had turned to family size and later to Cade, any more traditional ideas—ideas concerning deeper feelings—had taken a turn, and not for the better.

They hadn't seen eye-to-eye on the size of a family. Just as troubling, she'd as good as sided with Cade on the Bindy Rufus disaster. He'd been a little on edge ever since.

"Your bride is a charming young lady."

Brought back from his thoughts, Tristan turned from the small group of his university friends to a colleague, Don Schluter.

Despite his recent niggling misgivings, Tristan had to agree. "Yes, she is."

"She's a lucky woman, going from her position to marrying one of the most eligible bachelors in the country."

Tristan conceded, "It doesn't happen every day that the housekeeper marries her boss."

Don's brows fell together. "Not her position as a housekeeper."

Tristan wondered aloud. "Then you knew about her caring for her ill mother?"

"Well…no."

"Working in a doctor's surgery?"

"I mean *dating* a prominent doctor for a short time then having it all fall apart. My wife was a patient at the practice and got all the gossip. Today she recognized Ella straight off." Don shook his head. "Horrible business when he came to strife, losing it all over some scandal or another. Of course she had the good sense to get rid of him before that was finalized." Don's banter and smile dissolved. "Surely you knew."

Tristan blinked several times then remembered to breathe. "She mentioned…something."

Don shrank into his collar. "Perhaps I shouldn't have said anything."

Tristan glanced over. Ella was no longer talking with her friend.

A depraved idea struck, his stomach wrenched and he jerked a look around. But Cade hadn't shown his face here today.

For Pete's sake, what was he thinking? He trusted Ella. He couldn't be wrong about her character. So she'd had an affair with a doctor and left him when his career had stalled. That didn't make her a gold digger. And, no, perhaps she wasn't certain at this time about the size of a family. That didn't mean she'd lain in wait for months, seizing the right opportunity to introduce a miraculous makeover and, soon after that, a surprise pregnancy.

She wasn't that kind of woman.

A waiter interrupted his thoughts. "Excuse, Mr. Barkley. A gentleman asked if I could give you this. He wasn't able to stay."

Setting his glass in the crook of his arm, Tristan accepted an envelope and, preoccupied, tore open the seal then pulled out a black-and-white photograph. He took a double take at the revealing picture. Ella hugging tight a man of medium height and swarthy complexion. A man Tristan recognized.

Drago Scarpini.

Tristan gripped and bent the photo as his surroundings warped and creaked around him. Ella hated Scarpini. All this time he'd been trying to extort her. So why was he embracing her in this photo?

He stuffed the photo back into the envelope as his body began to burn.

He needed an explanation and he needed it now.

Tristan lodged his glass on a passing waiter's tray, then, in search of her, strode around the corner. Astounded, he stopped dead.

Cut off from the other guests, Ella stood at the end of a far garden, surrounded by scarlet creeping roses. Tristan had been just in time to witness Ella's half brother grab her face and kiss her—with more aggression than affection, but a kiss nonetheless.

Josh's voice broke into Tristan's consciousness, which was framed by a building red haze.

"Hey, there you are!"

Tristan swung around and put up his hand. "One minute, Josh—"

But when he wheeled back, both Scarpini and Ella had disappeared. He looked closer then took a few steps forward. What was this? A magician's trick!

Grace was with Josh. "Tristan…" she asked hesitantly. "Have you lost something?"

Dazed, Tristan ran a hand through his hair. "I'm… not sure."

"Some guests are getting ready to leave," Josh told him, "but before we head off, Grace and I wanted to ask what you'd like for a wedding gift. She says a honeymoon in Fiji, I say a home theatre. I know you have one, but with the latest technology the audio is amazing." Tristan felt Josh's hand on his arm. "Mate, is something wrong?" Josh asked in a lowered voice. "Did Cade show up after all?"

Tristan shook his head. "For once Cade had the good sense to do the right thing and stay away."

Grace stepped in. "Is Ella okay?"

Dumbfounded, Tristan huffed. "I really don't know anymore." When they both simply stared at him, Tristan rubbed his forehead and backtracked. He didn't want to alarm anyone. "Sorry. It's been a big week."

But even as he spoke, his mind wound back and forth over the possibilities.

If Ella was afraid of Scarpini, why was she talking to him—here of all places? Why were his arms around her in this photo? He remembered how reluctant she'd been to bring in the law. Could it be? Was it possible they were in on this extortion scheme together? Some warped plan to filter out his money. Perhaps Ella had wanted to shake Scarpini now that she was married, and this photograph was Scarpini's ammunition to bring a double-crosser down or bring her back into line.

Or was Ella once again merely an unwitting victim in this? But that didn't explain this photo. That embrace.

He, Josh and Grace moved back to the main area and Ella was there, saying goodbye to a friend. Tristan held tight the envelope, watching her movements through different eyes. He wouldn't condemn her—everyone deserved a fair trial.

Ella was wound up tighter than a spring by the time they arrived home that afternoon. Striding into what was now their bedroom, Tristan seemed just as uneasy.

His face a mask, he threw his jacket on the bed then peeled off his black jersey shirt. Without looking at her, he walked to the bedside table and emptied his pockets. Steadying herself, she leaned on a wall and slipped off her red high-heel shoes.

Tristan had been a little reserved since their wedding night when they'd discussed the size of families and, later, Cade and Bindy. But his mood now was something else again, and the reason was clear.

He must have seen her with Scarpini at the reception. Perhaps he'd even seen Scarpini take the most shocking of liberties. When she'd told him to go to hell, he'd forced a repugnant kiss on her mouth. The last time he'd tried a similar stunt, he'd also taken her off guard, but given those circumstances she hadn't made a scene. Today, however, she'd shoved him and darted away as fast as she could.

Now she crossed the room, sat beside Tristan on the edge of the bed and took a deep breath. He was upset that Scarpini had found out about today's celebration and had dared to show up. So was she.

"You saw Scarpini there today," she murmured.

Nodding, Tristan kept his eyes on his feet. "I saw you with him."

"He stayed only a minute, just long enough to laugh about your police friend's warning. He said nothing would stop him getting that money. He said now I have plenty to spare."

She shuddered remembering his blazing eyes, his cheap cologne and the way his mouth had quivered when he'd demanded that she listen.

She hugged herself against a sudden chill. "He seems so...*desperate.*" Scarpini had grabbed her arm so hard she knew she'd have a bruise tomorrow. After showing up so brazenly today, she couldn't guess what he was capable of.

"Tristan," she murmured, "he frightens me."

Tristan stood and measured her with his eyes. He didn't seem half as upset as she thought he would be. Rather, he looked wooden.

"You can lay charges," he said simply.

She supposed now there was no choice. "He said that the men he owes want more money. I didn't think I'd ever say this, everything tells me it's wrong, but... Maybe we should give him something more, just enough to get him out of the trouble he's in. Maybe then he'll leave us alone."

Wincing, she dropped her head in her hands and groaned. That wasn't the solution. She'd thought the same thing a hundred times over, and giving in to Scarpini's threats—even if he turned out to truly be her half brother—wasn't what needed to be done.

Tristan moved to the mirrored wardrobe and slid the door back. "I was thinking today about your position here as housekeeper." He pulled out a button-down she'd ironed that morning. "You never said who told you about this job."

Ella's brow pinched. Why was he changing the subject? "It was my mother. She mentioned it the day before she died."

"How did she find out about it?"

Ella remembered back. "She said a friend saw the position advertised in the classifieds. Her daughter was planning to apply."

"The agency didn't print my name," he said without emotion.

She tried to see past his mask. "I'm sorry, but they must have."

Buttoning his shirt, he sauntered back over. "Your mother must have been disappointed when your relationship with the doctor didn't pan out."

A twist of sick apprehension curled in her stomach. She didn't like his dead tone or the steely look that hardened his eyes.

"I went out with a doctor for a time," she freely admitted. "Where is all this going?"

"I spoke with a colleague today who knew him. Or rather, knew of your affair. He said the doctor lost everything."

Ella blinked several times, unable to absorb where this conversation was headed. "Sean was sued for malpractice. He drank. It caught up with him."

"So you decided to cut him loose?"

She bristled. "He drank more after the suit was filed. He blamed everyone but himself for his misfortune, including me."

"You seem to get yourself caught up with less than scrupulous characters."

"I misjudged him."

"And Scarpini?"

"I never wanted to have anything to do with him." Growing more indignant by the second, she lifted her chin. "Now do I get to hear about every affair you've ever had? I have a few hours."

Her fingers dug into the mattress either side of her. She hadn't meant to say that. But she didn't like his questioning, as if she hadn't deserved any kind of romantic life before he'd come along.

"How did Scarpini know to find you here?"

She shot to her feet. "Is this an inquisition?"

His eyes were cool. "Should it be?"

She crossed her arms. Fine. She'd answer his questions. "He said he got the name from the lawyer's receptionist. He told her he wanted to get in touch with his sister to thank her."

Tristan put his hands low on his hips. "I doubt any solicitor's employee is that stupid."

A withering feeling fell through her middle. "Tristan, what are you accusing me of?"

His eyes narrowed almost imperceptibly then he crossed to his jacket and pulled an envelope from the pocket. The photograph he slid out and displayed made Ella's stomach roil.

"Can you explain this?"

Her gaze lifted from the photo to the muscle jumping in his jaw. "Someone must have taken it at my mother's funeral."

"The funeral. Doesn't look as if you're running too hard from him here. In fact..." He studied the photo. "This is quite an embrace."

Her throat thickened. It wasn't how it looked. "I'd

just put my mother in the ground. Lots of people came up to console me. I could barely see through my tears."

He merely looked at her as if he was trying to see beneath the surface to something that just wasn't there—guilt.

"He sent this to you to cause trouble," she went on.

He huffed. "Yeah, well, it worked."

"He wants me to pay him off so he'll leave us alone."

Scarpini had told her not to push or he'd push back harder, and he'd been true to his word.

Expressionless, Tristan crushed the photo in his hand.

Her throat convulsed. "Tristan, don't you believe me? What other explanation is there?"

His narrowed eyes dimmed and then lowered. His hand with the photo dropped to his side. "Doesn't matter what I believe. I simply want this situation fixed. You're my wife. You're pregnant with my child."

She held her forehead, trying to fit the jumbled pieces together. "What you mean is you acted impulsively by marrying me and now you're paying for it."

"Don't put words in my mouth."

"Can you deny that's what you're thinking?"

He turned away from her. "We'll talk tomorrow when we have cooler heads."

Tears burned in her throat. She wanted to talk now. "I have a past, Tristan, and it's not squeaky clean. Neither is yours."

"I'm an open book. I don't hide behind anything."

"Then why haven't you come out and spoken to Cade about his sleeping with your ex?"

As he slowly turned back to her, his chin dropped along with his voice. "I don't need to lower myself."

"You said it…a man has choices, and you'd rather sooth your conscience by refusing to see the truth."

His nostrils flared. "Be careful with your next words, Ella."

She faltered, but she couldn't back down now.

"You haven't spoken to Cade because it suits you to blame him for Bindy's death. You have an excuse for your decision to abandon Barkley Hotels and go off to prove that you're bigger and better." She crossed her arms. "I don't believe Cade slept with Bindy and, deep down, I'd bet neither do you. You said she knew about his appendix scar. Could there be another explanation? Is it possible she'd ever seen Cade in a swimsuit?"

When he looked at her hard, frowned then blinked rapidly, she knew he'd remembered something connected.

Her shoulders went back. "I can't be sure why Bindy would've made up that affair. But I can guess. You'd begun to freeze her out like you're freezing me out now and she wanted to hurt you."

He scowled. "Don't twist things."

"If Cade is the villain you want to convince yourself he is, wouldn't he take pleasure in admitting the affair?"

"Not while he wants me to work for him."

"And that's the bottom line, isn't it? You're not prepared to work with him. It's your way or no way."

His jaw tightened. "I thought you understood the type of man I am."

"Seems we've been working at cross-purposes, then. You're the man who can't make a mistake so you wanted to believe I was perfect. I had this idea that I was only good enough to serve, so I put you on a pedestal like you were some kind of god—"

He threw up his hands and turned away again. "You're not talking sense."

She talked over him. "But the truth is we're both human."

They both deserved to be loved for who they were. She stopped to think that through and suddenly the understanding and decision seemed clear. Resolved, she headed for the door.

His voice followed her. "Ella, we're not finished."

Her throat aching, she turned at the door to face him. "I think we are."

He took a step closer. "What's that supposed to mean?"

"Tristan…" Her nose stung as her eyes welled up. "I thought I could, but I can't…I can't live like this."

She wasn't a chattel, or an automaton. She had emotions. She needed to belong and to be loved and believed. She knew now that Tristan would never acknowledge that.

His eyes flashed before turning to cool black stone. "If you're planning on doing something rash…if you're thinking for one moment of divorce…" His throat bobbed then his jaw clenched. "I'm the father of that baby. I'll do what I have to."

"I know you will." She walked away before he could see the tears. "So will I."

Eleven

Early the next morning, Ella emerged from her downstairs bedroom to the sound of oil hissing in a pan and the smell of warm toast.

Tristan stood at the hot plates, naked from the waist up, a towel wrapped around his hips, a spatula in his hand. Sunshine streaming through the window lit his body from behind, leaving a silver halo around his bronzed, masculine frame. She almost sighed.

He glanced up from the pan and smiled hesitantly. "Good morning."

She frowned and, head down, moved forward. "You're cooking?"

"Eggs and mushrooms."

She inspected the pan as she passed. Nothing

burned. But she didn't offer to take over. Instead she crossed to the fridge and found the pitcher of juice.

Tristan returned to his work. "Would you like some?"

"No thanks."

He turned on the charm with a crooked grin. "I can vouch they'll at least be edible."

"I'm not hungry."

The pan hissed more. While he flipped eggs, she retrieved a glass, refusing to give in and ogle at the way his muscles worked down and across the broad expanse of his back. His hair was mussed. A lock bobbed on his forehead and his biceps flexed as he scraped to ease the egg from the pan.

He'd never looked more handsome.

"Did you sleep last night?" he asked.

Snapping back to reality, she averted her gaze and poured the juice. "I don't want to do this right now."

"You don't want to talk?"

"I can't pretend that what happened yesterday didn't."

Juice in hand she started back toward her former bedroom. She had a busy day ahead. She needed to get dressed.

His deep voice followed her. "I've had a chance to think things through."

Her stomach lurched and she gripped the glass tighter. "Let me guess. You've decided that you can live with your mistake if it means keeping your child."

"I've decided I may have jumped to conclusions."

At her door, she turned to face him. "And suddenly everything is better."

"I'm trying to mend things." Oil splattered in the pan. Growling, he jumped back, rubbing his six-pack where it must have hit and burned.

He looked like such a wonderful contradiction, for once out of his depth yet still master of his environment.

"Want to know something?" she murmured, almost without thinking.

He grabbed a tea towel and rubbed himself again. "I'm hopeless in the kitchen?"

"I love you."

His gaze shot up to find hers.

"I hadn't told you before," she went on, "because like a schoolgirl I was waiting for you to say it first. Marrying you was like a fantastic dream come true for me. But last night told me one important and very sad thing. For whatever reason, you feel trapped. As much as I'd like to pretend and tell myself you'll grow to love me, too—"

Her heart squeezed, but she found a resigned smile and shrugged. "I don't believe it anymore. And I can't live like that...not for all the money in the world."

"Ella—"

He started forward, but she stepped back.

"Please respect me enough not to patronize me and say you love me now. I deserve more. From this point on I'm going to put myself and my baby's needs first." She took a moment to be sure of her words. "And I'm not certain bringing up a child in this environment is best."

His brows fell together. "You don't know what you're saying."

"My father only ever treated my mother with respect, even after the accident. When she came out of her coma, she was still kind and loving but…different. Slower. But it didn't matter to my father. That's love. I won't settle for less."

His gaze lowered as he thought it over and he nodded, although she didn't believe he'd accepted her decision. When Tristan Barkley wanted something, he didn't give in easily.

Leaving him, she closed her bedroom door and headed for her wardrobe. Now she had to deal with Scarpini and knew exactly what to do. Go to the police. She should have done it a long time ago.

She heard the bedroom door thrust open. She spun around and Tristan was standing in the doorway, proud, tall, fire glinting his eyes.

His voice was low and rough with determination. "I can't let this end."

She stood her ground while her heart thudded madly in her chest. "This time you don't get to choose."

"You need to listen to me."

Two long strides and he caught her upper arms. Her body betrayed her, reacting to his touch, begging her to lean into him and believe he was the husband she wanted him to be—trusting and wholly in love with his wife.

Finding the strength, she put her palms against his chest. "A marriage can't be a business arrangement. Not my marriage, anyway. I can't live in the same house knowing that I'm not the convenience you wanted to find."

He focused on her lips. "Ella, you know how I feel about you."

Yes, she knew. She was supposed to have been everything he'd wanted in a wife. She'd fit the bill. But now he'd found out that she was a woman with a past and regrets like everyone else. And she hated him for wanting her to be more than human. Yet when his grip tightened on her arms and his mouth grazed her brow, that knowledge seemed to evaporate as she trembled with traitorous desire.

She meant to push against his bare chest, but instead her fingers kneaded hot, tensed muscle. "This won't change my mind. I already know we're compatible in the bedroom."

"This isn't compatible. It's *combustible*." His mouth trailed her temple, as his hand, moving to her behind, urged her body firmly against his. "Tell me you don't want me," he murmured against her cheek, against her lips, "Tell me and I'll go."

She wanted to, so desperately, but the words wouldn't form in her mind. Her thoughts were consumed by images and sensations that left her speechless. When his hands slid up to ease the robe from her shoulders, she felt too weak to do anything but sway.

"Tristan…"

"We're man and wife. You belong to me as much as I belong to you. That's what you're feeling now. What you can't resist."

She felt his towel drop from around his hips to their feet then sighed when his mouth covered and claimed hers.

Kissing her deeply, he walked her back toward the bed. She wanted to tell him to leave and yet a voice in her head whispered that this was the last time. The last time she kissed him, held him, made love to the man she would love forever.

"Well, this is a surprise."

Sitting in the stands of a vacant baseball field, Tristan glanced up at his visitor. An hour had passed since he'd followed Ella into her bedroom, since they'd made love with an energy and desperation he'd never experienced before. He'd believed he could talk her around. Convince her to stay. Instead, afterward she'd dressed and coolly asked him to leave.

Her face had been so set, he'd known it wasn't the time to push further. But he'd have gone crazy waiting for the chance to speak with and touch her again. So he'd made a phone call and had come here.

Now Tristan nodded at his brother, who had made it in record time.

"Thanks for coming, Cade."

In jeans and a black T-shirt, Cade took a seat beside him. "As if I wouldn't. What's up?"

Tristan leaned back, resting his elbows on the slats behind. The words came remarkably easily. "Josh is right. This feud needs to end."

Tristan heard Cade's sharp intake of air. After a protracted pause, Cade exhaled on a broad smile. "I can't tell you how glad I am to hear that."

Tristan forced himself to look into his brother's eyes—eyes he'd thought he'd grown to hate but now realized he'd only envied.

"If you want to know the truth…all these years I resented your success."

Cade scoffed. "My success? Sorry, but is this the class captain five years running talking? And if I recall you currently own one of the most successful property development businesses in the country." Arching a brow, Cade leaned back, too. "I think we're at least even in the success stakes."

"But you've never had to try." Tristan lowered his gaze. "I can't take my eye off the ball for a minute."

Cade laced his hands between his thighs. "I'll tell you a secret, one you already know. Inheriting money is one thing, but no one hands success to you on a platter. You have to work damn hard for it, make the right decisions—" his knuckles turned white as he clasped his hands tighter "—and sometimes be prepared to know you've made the wrong decision and still move forward."

Tristan exhaled. He'd known this was coming and he was prepared to concede. "You're talking about my wanting to refurbish."

Cade nodded. "I owe you an apology."

Tristan's mouth dropped open. *"What?"*

"You were right. We should have refurbished those hotels. It could have got us back on track much sooner. But I was scared witless we'd get ourselves in too much debt. I chickened out and the board is always ready to agree to the safe option."

Tristan tried to absorb the admission and apology. He'd lain awake some nights anticipating this kind of turnaround, but he'd never truly believed this day would come.

Cade continued. "I was tough on you, Tristan. Too tough. I only had the best interests of the company at heart, but I didn't blame you when you walked."

Tristan gave in to a grin and, leaning sideways, knocked his shoulder against Cade's like he used to when they'd been young. "Well, thanks for that. It means a lot."

"I should have said it sooner."

"Except I wouldn't let you anywhere near me."

Cade chuckled. "There was that." His expression sobered. "But a lot of things have changed. The biggest being Josh shares the chair now. If you came back on board, decisions could be made based on unanimous vote or best out of three. We wouldn't need to arm-wrestle every play."

Tristan went through the last two decades in his mind—their youth, the tumultuous time working together, what he'd achieved on his own.

He cocked his head. "Let me think about it."

Cade stuck out his hand. "That's all I ask. You'd be a fantastic asset to our company."

Tristan doubled back. "*Our* company?"

"The three of us," Cade confirmed. "You, me and Josh. That'll never change."

As Tristan studied his brother, his insides looped. Should he ask Cade about Bindy? he wondered.

But he didn't need to. Cade was big enough to admit that he'd been wrong about the refurbishment issue, and Tristan was big enough to admit that Ella had been right about so many things.

Cade might be ruthless in the business world, and he might look like their old man, but no way was he like him—not as far as cheating was concerned. When Ella had kept digging, he'd remembered that Bindy had seen Cade by the pool once briefly, but obviously she'd taken notes. Her wild accusation of Cade's seduction had been just that—a story he'd been all too willing to believe.

But that supposed betrayal had ratified Tristan's decision to break out into business on his own—to prove himself without feeling as if he were crawling out from beneath big brother's shadow and deserting the family business. He needed to acknowledge that now.

"Cade, there's something else I need to say." Lord, how to start? "I let myself believe someone's lies and it colored my view about you even more."

Cade clasped Tristan's hand and smiled. "Enough said. Let's just let bygones be bygones."

Perhaps Cade had somehow found out about Bindy's accusation, or maybe he was simply happier to let go of the bad feelings without more explanation. Either way, if Cade didn't want him to push, Tristan wouldn't.

Cade sat back again, squinting into the noonday mirages simmering over the baseball diamond. "We should drop by Josh's and tell him the news."

Tristan shook his head. "Not today. I have some major groveling to do."

"Don't tell me…your first marital spat?"

"It's a doozy."

Cade sucked air in between his teeth. "Can't help there. I'm a confirmed bachelor. But one piece of advice might fit. If you want something, work hard enough and you'll get it."

Tristan gazed at the empty baseball field. He didn't want complications. He wanted predictability, smooth sailing, an easy life. But he also wanted to protect and care for Ella, and be a real father to their baby.

Predictability.

Ella.

One cancelled out the other. So how the hell could he have both?

Twelve

Ella eased out a relieved sigh and smiled as she spoke into the phone receiver.

"Thank you, Mrs. Shelby. You've been a great help."

As Ella disconnected, a terrific wave of vindication rolled through her.

After Tristan had left, she'd pulled herself together enough to make a couple of phone calls. Just now she'd contacted her mother's friend. She hadn't seen an advertisement. Seemed her daughter had known the housekeeper Tristan had just let go and heard about the job that week.

Ella had also contacted the lawyer's office to inquire whether the receptionist had indeed given Scarpini her phone number. The new receptionist promptly transferred her to a junior partner who explained they'd needed to let the previous receptionist go; was there any matter she wished to discuss?

Ella declined. A complaint now would accomplish nothing. The junior partner's inference was good enough for her. If the receptionist had been less than competent, she could very well have erroneously given out personal details. While that settled the issue in Ella's mind—Scarpini had told the truth about how he'd obtained her phone number—she couldn't make up Tristan's mind for him.

Neither could she forget the look in his eyes when he'd shown her the photo of Scarpini stealing an embrace at Roslyn's funeral. When he'd rushed into his proposal, Tristan had envisaged a worry-free married life. Instead he'd got her. How he must curse the day he'd ever assumed that they'd make a "good pair."

The intercom buzzed and, shaken from her thoughts, Ella crossed to the communication panel on the wall. Her stomach muscles tensed as she reached for the button.

Oh, but she was tired of Scarpini's sinister cloud hanging over her. If he was brazen enough to show up at the gate, dammit, he could bring on his worst. Her next phone call was going to be to the police, anyway.

She depressed a button and her greeting was harsh. "What do you want?"

The intercom snapped back. "Ella, it's Grace. Can I come through?"

Ella slumped and opened the gates.

A moment later, Grace was at the front door, her pretty face pale with worry. "I hope you don't mind me dropping in like this."

"Of course not." In truth, Ella was glad of the company. "Can I get you anything?"

Grace laid her light jacket on the sideboard. "How about a zip for my mouth?"

Ella linked her arm through Grace's and led her down the hall. "What's happened?"

"Josh and I had our first quarrel."

"About the wedding arrangements?"

Big weddings were known to cause all kinds of differences. Who to invite, what cars to hire, whether the in-laws would cause any heartache—not that Ella had had to worry about those things when Tristan had sped her off to New Zealand. She'd chosen a gown, he'd organized the paperwork, they'd said their vows and that had been that. Done and dusted.

Grace lifted a coy gaze. "We argued about you and Tristan."

Ella frowned. "I don't understand."

As they entered the kitchen, Grace rushed it out. "We sensed the vibes at the end of the day yesterday. Things between the two of you were obviously strained. I wondered if it was something to do with the reception. If anything had upset you, I wanted to know. But Josh said to butt out. He doesn't understand that sometimes women need to talk things through."

Ella poured two coffees. "Men are different."

They were "doers," always ready for action, whereas females were more likely to rely on language. She wished she'd spoken more to Tristan about his proposal. But he'd seemed so certain, and she'd felt so strongly about him for so long. Then, when she'd found out about her pregnancy…

Her stomach knotted and she looked down at her tummy.

Her innocent baby was stuck in the middle.

They sat at a wrought iron table, the warm sun on their skin easing the strain. After Grace got a few grumbles off her chest, she came to the conclusion that Josh had been a little short with her because he believed Tristan would come to him if he needed to talk.

Then Ella confessed that she and Tristan were going through a rough patch because of a man from her past, but she didn't go into detail. She didn't want Grace to know how serious the situation had become. It would only worry her more.

An hour later, they were at the door, hugging and saying goodbye. As Ella wandered back inside, she smiled, knowing she was lucky to have Grace as a sister-in-law. No matter what happened between herself and Tristan, Josh and Grace would always be her baby's uncle and aunt. No matter what came, she wouldn't deprive anyone of seeing their family.

Wincing, she caught her forehead in her palm.

Oh God, she didn't want to think about divorce. But she simply couldn't go through life living with a man who valued her cooking over her heart.

Another knock on the door brought her back. Her gaze landed on Grace's jacket, still on the sideboard.

Understanding, she grabbed the jacket and called out, "Coming."

But when she opened the door, the garment slipped from her hand as dread drained through her like a poison.

Drago Scarpini didn't bother with pleasantries. He elbowed the door open and pushed his way inside.

"I'm leaving the country," he announced, looking around the pristine interior of the vestibule with a deep scowl on his face.

Willing her breathing and her racing heart to calm, Ella folded her arms. "Good."

"And you're going to give me a parting gift."

He named a price and Ella recoiled. "That's my entire inheritance."

He grabbed her arm. "Don't forget, as compensation for getting rid of me, you receive a hassle-free lifetime with Richie Rich."

She wrenched her arm free. "You can't intimidate me."

Contempt blazed in his eyes. "Miss high and mighty. You think you're so much better because you grew up with the nice family. You had my father while I had to listen to my grandparents refer to their only grandson as *the bastard.*"

Ella cringed.

"I got by," he explained as his spicy cologne assaulted her senses. "But I won't be satisfied until that man repays just a little of what he took from me when he left. And you're going to help me."

"You can't blame my father for not knowing he had a son."

Scarpini's hateful mouth turned down. "Jump in my shoes and maybe you can." He yanked her arm again. "So let's sort this matter out once and for all."

He dragged her down the hall, shuffled her into the kitchen and came across her handbag.

"Is this where you keep you checkbook, or is it in a drawer somewhere?" He wildly spun around. "Your bedroom maybe."

"No!" She tugged back. She didn't want any other man near there, particularly Scarpini. Beaten for the moment, feeling his hold tighten mercilessly on her arm, she ground out, "The checkbook's in my bag."

Grabbing the underside of the bag, he shook it and dumped everything out. Her brush clattered to the tiles, a lipstick twirled across the counter. Desperation drawing down his face, Scarpini trawled through the jumble and found his treasure.

A lewd grin crept over his face before he flicked the checkbook at her over the counter. "Write it to cash. And so you can't make any nasty phone calls, you're coming down to the bank with me."

She clenched her jaw in a bid to stop the shaking. "I won't do it."

"Sign. The." He slammed his fist on the counter. *"Check!"*

Jumping, she took in his crimson face, the dark warning simmering in his eyes. She closed her own eyes and prayed.

"No."

She yelped when he yanked her through the back doors and outside. With the checkbook scrunched in his hand, he forced her to kneel. As the gravel bit into her knees, he whipped out a gun from his coat pocket and held it to her forehead. Ella almost blacked out as a wave of light-headedness swept over her.

The cold metal nudged her brow. "You have a choice to make, *bella*. Make it the right one."

Fighting the nausea pushing up the back of her throat, Ella opened her mouth to speak. The growl of an engine rolling up the drive stemmed the words. She could have laughed out loud with relief.

Then she remembered the gun and her surroundings receded as the possibilities narrowed down to one.

Reading her expression, Scarpini grinned and repositioned his gun, aiming its shiny barrel at the back doors.

"Sign your name now, let me cash the check and I won't put a bullet through his head. And before you think of doing anything foolish—like trying to warn him—please know my solemn vow. If I don't succeed now, if you do anything to stop me from getting that money, I'll come back and finish the job."

Tristan parked his car in the garage, his thoughts crowded with his discussion with Cade, but more with how he should approach this crucial time with Ella.

She'd been right. In a way he had felt trapped, but it was a cage of his own making, built on pride and stubbornness.

How could he make this work? How could he make *them* work?

As he entered the kitchen, his step faltered and his frown grew. Her handbag was on the counter…dumped upside down as it had been once before. Fine-tuning every sense, he slowly eased around, his gut wrenching tighter as he completed a full circle.

He'd nearly panicked the first time he'd come across a similar scene. He'd been wrong about the situation, like he'd been wrong about so many things. But this time—today—felt different.

His nose lifted on a scent. Perfume?

The hair on the back of his neck prickled.

No, cologne. Something cheap.

He pricked up his ears… No sound. He crept to the living room and saw nothing untoward. But this intuition—the deep-seated sensation that something was very wrong—wasn't his imagination. He moved quietly to the side window and painstakingly pulled back a blade of the blind to get an angled view of the back lawn.

His heart jumped then crashed madly against his ribs. He had to bite his lip to stifle a growl of blind fury. Ella was on her knees and that lowlife, Scarpini, had a gun. Not aimed at her, but at the back door, anticipating *his* movements.

Tristan's hand curled into a deadly fist.

She'd said Scarpini was desperate and he'd dismissed it. Now he was paying the ultimate price. But this battle was far from over. That mongrel not only had his wife, he was holding Tristan's unborn child hostage.

As he watched, Ella scribbled something, and Tristan honed his vision. A checkbook? But how did Scarpini think he would get away with this? Or maybe that didn't matter anymore. Maybe Scarpini wanted this to end and he didn't care how.

Tristan slid away from the window and gathered his intelligence. But he didn't have time to sift through every scenario. He had to act quickly or that gun might go off and Ella was the closest target.

He threw a glance toward the kitchen door.

He'd left the garage door open. Grabbing an orange from the fruit bowl, he focused to calm his voice, pretending to suspect nothing so as to put Scarpini off his game.

"Hey, Ella! You here?"

No reply, of course, although he might have expected Scarpini to have her answer to lure him outside—a sitting duck for target practice.

Tristan crept out of the kitchen, through the garage. Counting each heartbeat, he stalked along the side of the house until he edged his nose around the corner. Ella's head was down, resigned but also courageous.

The woman he loved.

The woman Tristan knew in that moment he would always love and be willing to die for.

Scarpini had his back to Tristan. With the check in one hand, the gun in the other, Scarpini held his gaze on the back door and began to reverse—one step, then two—no doubt hoping to escape. Tristan stepped out into the open, took aim then filled his lungs to capacity and called out.

"Scarpini!"

The other man whirled around. Tristan had barely enough time to register the shock on his face before he pitched the orange. At the same time the orange hit Scarpini's hand, the gun went off. Leaping into action, Ella scrambled and dived on the gun. With shaking hands, she leveled it at Scarpini.

She chanced a glance to her right and quivered out a thankful smile. "You've got quite an arm there."

Rushing over, Tristan took the gun from her, his eyes on Scarpini the whole time. "Thanks," he replied, and then unclipped the cell phone from his belt. "Call the police."

She brushed her knees and took the phone. "With pleasure."

Tristan spoke to a sneering Scarpini, who had grudgingly raised his hands in the air. "And you...don't twitch a muscle. At this range I can't miss." Tristan grinned. "And, believe me, I don't want to."

Thirteen

Later that day, Ella stood at the front door beside Tristan as he bid his police friend, Detective Sergeant William Peters, goodbye.

Tristan shook the sergeant's hand. "Thanks, Bill. I appreciate you taking care of this."

"It'll give me the greatest pleasure to make sure every document and shred of evidence is locked in. This creep won't get out of a hefty prison term." His chin came down. "I'll see you both down at the station tomorrow morning for your statements."

Tristan nodded. "Bright and early."

The sergeant spoke to Ella. "Afternoon, Mrs. Barkley." He tipped his head. "You're a gutsy lady."

As Tristan closed the door, Ella tried to fathom what would come next. Today had been a tumult of emotion and activity. It was difficult to believe the long, tragic episode with Scarpini was finally over.

But there was another problem to solve—her marriage to Tristan. She was sick to her stomach for it, but she couldn't see any solution. If she couldn't be any more to Tristan than a glorified housekeeper, her conscience, her heart, her very soul told her she had to say goodbye.

He faced her, so tall and invincible…her every primal urge cried out for the strength of those arms to enfold her. She'd never forget that he'd saved her today. Unfortunately, his act of bravery wasn't enough to save their marriage.

As if reading her thoughts, he slid his hands into his pockets. "You must be exhausted."

She exhaled some of the tension. "You'd think so. Must be adrenaline, but I feel as if I could climb a mountain."

"Are you up to a drive?"

She hurried to shake her head. "I don't think that would be a good idea."

"Let's try it and see."

She thought of refusing again, but his eyes held a certain emotion she hadn't seen before. And he had come to her rescue in the most swashbuckling way.

She let out a sigh.

Oh hell, after that harrowing ordeal she could admit she'd still like Tristan close for just a little longer.

When they were in his car, Tristan cruised out onto the open street. After a few minutes of uneasy silence, Tristan admitted, "I saw Cade today."

Her head snapped toward him. "He called you?"

"Other way around. Ella, I might not have wanted to hear it, but you made me face a lot of things I'd tried to ignore in the past."

He sounded completely humbled, entirely sincere. Different from the defensive man who'd refused to listen yesterday, or the persuasive force she'd succumbed to this morning.

"You were right," he said. "I wanted to believe the worst so I could justify my self-righteous departure from Barkley Hotels. I told Cade as much today."

A smile eased across her face. If nothing else, this episode had got two brothers, who deep down cared greatly about each other, talking again.

"Are you going back to work for Barkley's?"

His jaw shifted. "I haven't decided yet. It's not totally out of the question."

"Do you really believe you could work together? You've been on your own for a while."

"You mean if I'm not prepared to budge on the marina to feather my own nest, it's unlikely I'll go for a three-way split of power between me, Josh and Cade?"

Familiar tension gripped between her shoulders. "I shouldn't have asked."

He kept his eyes on the road. "Let's try to enjoy the drive."

Her stomach churning, Ella looked blankly out the window. If Tristan didn't want to talk, she wouldn't push. Rather, she would try to enjoy his company, albeit pensive. She'd need to face reality, and their separation, soon enough.

She wasn't surprised when they turned into the road

that led to Tristan's prize parcel of land. He pulled up close to where the parkland met the white sand and glistening blue sea.

When they alighted, the breeze was mild and warm, the setting sun throwing back a smoky rose-gold glow over the endless horizon.

"Still think this is paradise?" he asked.

"Who wouldn't?" she replied. "You'll make a lot of money when it's developed."

"I'd rather have you."

She swung her glance from the rolling waves to his profile. She knew he wanted her. But wanting and loving weren't the same thing. And she couldn't stay in a relationship where only one person loved the other. It was a formula for heartache. In Tristan's mother's case, it had been a recipe for disaster.

"You said once you wanted to live here." His gaze found hers. "I'm giving it to you."

Did he think that this was the answer to keeping her, keeping their child? It wasn't.

"What about your deal and Mayor Rufus? You were near desperate to get that rezoning."

"After I left Cade today, I phoned the mayor. I let him know I was happy to give him the land he needs to develop the marina, but I didn't need the rezoning on the portion that we would retain. I want to build our family home here."

Pain struck her chest like an arrow. She had to look down, away from his searching eyes. "Tristan, please, don't…"

"I'm sorry, Ella," he said in a low, steady voice. "I'm sorry for not appreciating you for everything you are. I'm sorry for doubting you. This trouble between us isn't your fault. It's mine."

"Because you normally only bet on sure things," she finished flatly.

Tristan's face said he didn't agree. "I trusted you from the moment we met. I've told you…you felt right in every way, like no other woman or person I've ever known. I should never have doubted that instinct. I should've simply let myself go and believe." He faced her fully, taking her hands in his much larger ones. "I can't blame you if you can't forgive me, but I'm asking you to give me another chance. For us. For our child."

His words were heartfelt. His warm hands holding hers filled her with tingling want and need. But no matter how wonderful all he'd said might sound, he still hadn't fully committed to her, and there could be only one reason why.

He couldn't say the magic words because if he did, she'd see the lie in his eyes.

"There's something else." He pulled a small, wrapped box from his trouser pocket. She shook her head—this wasn't the time for gifts. But he placed the box in her hand. "Please. Open it."

Feeling drained, she gave in, unwrapped the box, opened the lid and was struck nearly speechless. The stones were dazzling.

"Tristan, they're beautiful." Sapphires.

She remembered his words on their wedding day.

Was this the gift he'd wanted her to wear on their fiftieth anniversary? she wondered.

Mesmerized, she slipped one earring from its velvet

bed and twirled the jewel in the last of the sunlight. "They're the color of the ocean shallows at noon."

"They're the color of your eyes. I love your eyes." He brought her close. "Ella, I love you."

Her vision misted over as her throat swelled with emotion. She couldn't bear to look into his face for fear of what she might see.

He tilted up her chin. His eyes were clear and true. "Look into your heart—trust your instincts."

A hot tear slid down her cheek and around her jaw. Her heart was beating so madly, she could barely catch her breath. "You do?" You *really* do?

His thumb grazed her parted lips. "So much, it hurts."

A happy sob escaped. He couldn't have made that up, because she felt the exact same way.

Bouncing up on tiptoe, she wove her arms around his neck. Holding on tight, she murmured against his ear, "I love you, too."

And when he kissed her, it felt as if she always had.

But a thought struck and she pulled away quickly. "Tristan, do you still want seven children?" She wasn't prepared to hold back anything. Not ever again.

"Weren't you listening?" His smile was easy. "I want *you*."

"You're not just saying that now?" Perhaps he would change his mind and regret it later.

His brow pinched slightly. "I had this perfect illusion going on in my head—me with an old-fashioned gal taking care of several polite, well-behaved kids. I would come home at the end of every working day and pat each on the head before tucking them in bed." He shrugged. "I much prefer what we'll have together."

"What's that?"

"A family who understands about commitment and patience, openness and love, no matter how many members we end up with."

She breathed in, absorbing the fresh, salty air and as much of this magical moment as she could. "And you'd give up this land—a fortune—if it made me happy?"

"Without losing a wink of sleep." His mouth dropped over hers again. This time his kiss lifted her beyond any heights she could have imagined.

When he gently broke away, he peered into her eyes. "Ella, be mine. Be mine forever."

Her palm slid from around his neck to cup his jaw. "Only forever?"

His eyes crinkled at the corners before his warm lips brushed hers again. "That'll do for starters."

Epilogue

Ahead of the newlywed couple, Ella moved with the rest of the bridal party out onto the church steps. With the jubilant guests streaming out behind, Josh stopped to kiss his bride, theatrically tipping Grace back until her leg kicked up, sending her white tulle hem flying in a ruffling wave.

Standing apart from the applauding crowd, an orchid bouquet clasped to her chest, Ella first laughed then let out a sigh. A memorable ending to a moving ceremony. What could top two people declaring before friends and family their love for each other forever?

From behind, a deep voice near Ella's ear chased delicious tingles over her skin.

"Mmm, that looks good," he murmured, referring to the kiss. "Wanna try it?"

Ella smiled as Tristan turned her in the loving circle of his arms. Gathering her close, he kissed her with the right amount of passion mingled with the perfect balance of restraint. Not that there was a dire need for decorum. All eyes were on the beautiful bride and her enamored groom, who were smiling for an avalanche of photographs.

Ella ignored the flashes. At this moment, amid streaming jets of confetti bubbles, all she wanted to know—all she needed to feel—was the blissful security of her husband's arms. Whenever he was near, her world was complete.

Softly Tristan broke the kiss, looked deeply into her eyes then toyed with one of her sapphire eardrops.

Still floating from the effects of his embrace, she arched a teasing brow. "You like?"

"Yeah, I like." He touched her nose with his and smiled. "The earrings are okay, too." His fingertip trailed her throat. "I think I'm in love."

She melted more. "You'll never know how good that sounds."

The happy couple appeared at their side and Josh extended his hand to his brother. "Well, that went off well, don't you think?"

Tristan shook Josh's hand and brushed a kiss against Grace's cheek. "As a matter of fact, we're so impressed, we're planning on having a big day of our own."

Ella pulled a wry face. "Tristan, we're already married."

"But we didn't do it like this." Tristan squeezed her hand. "I was in such a hurry to make you my wife I deprived you of a day like today. We should do it again, this time with all the bells and whistles."

Ella couldn't speak. Their ceremony and been special but very private. Enjoying a wedding day with all the trimmings would be better than wonderful.

Bursting with excitement at the news, Grace leaned forward to kiss Tristan's cheek. "You are so thoughtful." Grace kissed Ella next. "Now I can return the favor and be your maid of honor."

"When you've sorted out the date," Josh said, leading his bride away, "join us for photographs. We're heading off in ten."

"Oh, and Ella," Grace got in. "You know the magazine I work for? The editor wants to talk to you about contacts."

Ella shrugged. "Contacts?"

"For publishing that cookbook when you've finished."

Grace gave a wink then disappeared back into the crowd with Josh, emerging at the other side where the stretch limousine waited.

All the more excited, Ella began to move off, too, but Tristan held her back.

His warm lips nuzzled her temple. "I just have to let you know…you're driving me wild in that dress. What say we leave early from the reception?"

She shivered as familiar heat unfurled through her bloodstream.

"We can't do that. You're best man."

"Cade can take over my duties." He slid a speculative look to his left. "Although big brother does seem a little preoccupied."

Ella glanced over. Near the limousine, Cade was deep in conversation with his partnered bridesmaid, a brunette with flashing blue eyes and curves few men could resist.

Tristan chuckled. "Seems bachelor boy is smitten. Perhaps we'll see their wedding day next."

"Imagine…all three brothers hitched."

Although he maintained his own business concerns, Tristan was a consultant for Barkley Hotels, and the brothers knew they were there for each other whenever and wherever needed.

How different Tristan's sibling situation was from her own. It was still difficult to believe she and Scarpini were related. After his arrest, he'd refused to consent to a DNA test, so she'd hired a private investigator, who confirmed through his inquiry that her father had indeed sired Drago Scarpini.

Sensing her train of thought, Tristan's brows nudged together. "If you are agonizing over Scarpini, don't. He's in jail and will be for a long time to come. He won't hurt you again."

She pressed her lips together. "I know. I just wish things had been different."

"You're not responsible for him, Ella. He had choices, like the rest of us. And speaking of choices…" His frown eased. "I'll never stop thanking God you chose me." He fanned his palm over her second-trimester tummy. "How long now?"

She couldn't help but laugh. "Same as when you asked this morning. Four months to go."

"You're going to make the best mother."

Her heart grew at the note of raw pride in his voice. "I'll try my best."

"You won't need to try. You're a natural. I've never been more certain of anything in my life."

"Then maybe we should think about having another one."

His eyes widened. "Another baby?"

She hitched up a shoulder. "It would be good to have another close to our first."

Ella had given it lots of thought. She would've loved a little sister or brother growing up. She wouldn't let her episode with Scarpini change her mind about what a family should be.

He cupped her cheek, the pad of his thumb grazing the slight cleft in her chin. "Count me in on all baby-making practice, but as far as extending our family—that's only *if* and *when* you're ready. I've learned to be thankful for what I hold most dear. I'll never risk losing either of you again."

Grateful tears sprang to her eyes as she placed her palm on his chest. "I love you, Tristan…so very much."

His dark eyes glistened. "Not nearly as much as I love you."

Feeling as light as the bubbles dancing around their heads, Ella surrendered to her husband's kiss, knowing fairy tales could and *did* come true.

* * * * *

Celebrate 60 years of pure reading
pleasure with Harlequin®!

Harlequin Presents® is proud to introduce its
gripping new miniseries,
THE ROYAL HOUSE OF KAREDES.
An exquisite coronation diamond, split as a symbol
of a warring royal family's feud, is missing! But
whoever reunites the diamond halves will rule all....

Welcome to eight brand-new titles that unfold to
reveal the stories of kings and queens, princes and
princesses torn apart by pride and power, but finally
reunited by love.

Step into the world of Karedes with
BILLIONAIRE PRINCE, PREGNANT MISTRESS
Available July 2009 from Harlequin Presents®.

ALEXANDROS KAREDES, SNOW DUSTING the shoulders of his leather jacket and glittering like jewels in his dark hair, stood at the door. Maria felt the blood drain from her head.

"Good evening, Ms. Santos."

His voice was as she remembered it. Deep. Husky. Perfect English, but with the faintest hint of a Greek accent. And cold, as cold as it had been that awful morning she would never forget, when he'd accused her of horrible things, called her terrible names...

"Aren't you going to ask me in?"

She fought for composure. Last time they'd faced each other, they'd been on his turf. Now they were on hers. She was in command here, and that meant everything.

"There's a sign on the door downstairs," she said, her

tone every bit as frigid as his. "It says, 'No soliciting or vagrants.'"

His lips drew back in a wolfish grin. "Very amusing."

"What do you want, Prince Alexandros?"

A tight smile eased across his mouth and it killed her that even now, knowing he was a vicious, arrogant man, she couldn't help but notice what a handsome mouth it was. Chiseled. Generous. Beautiful, like the rest of him, which made him living proof that beauty could, indeed, be only skin deep.

"Such formality, Maria. You were hardly so proper the last time we were together."

She knew his choice of words was deliberate. She felt her face heat; she couldn't help that but she damned well didn't have to let him lure her into a verbal sparring match.

"I'll ask you once more, your highness. What do you want?"

"Ask me in and I'll tell you."

"I have no intention of asking you in. Tell me why you're here or don't. It's your choice, just as it will be my choice to shut the door in your face."

He laughed. It infuriated her but she could hardly blame him. He was tall—six two, six three—and though he stood with one shoulder leaning against the door frame, hands tucked casually into the pockets of the jacket, his pose was deceptive. He was strong, with the leanly muscled body of a well-trained athlete.

She remembered his body with painful clarity. The feel of him under her hands. The power of him moving over her. The taste of him on her tongue.

Suddenly, he straightened, his laughter gone. "I have not come this distance to stand in your doorway," he said coldly, "and I am not going to leave until I am ready to do so. I suggest you stand aside and stop behaving like a petulant child."

A petulant child? Was that what he thought? This man who had spent hours making love to her and had then accused her of—of trading her body for profit?

Except it had not been love, it had been sex. And the sooner she got rid of him, the better.

She let go of the doorknob and stepped aside. "You have five minutes."

He strolled past her, bringing cold air and the scent of the night with him. She swung toward him, arms folded. He reached past her, pushed the door closed, then folded his arms, too. She wanted to open the door again but she'd be damned if she was going to get into a who's-in-charge-here argument with him. She was in charge, and he would surely see a tussle over the ground rules as a sign of weakness.

Instead, she looked past him at the big clock above her work table.

"Ten seconds gone," she said briskly. "You're wasting time, your highness."

"What I have to say will take longer than five minutes."

"Then you'll just have to learn to economize. More than five minutes, I'll call the police."

Instantly, his hand was wrapped around her wrist. He tugged her toward him, his dark-chocolate eyes almost black with anger.

"You do that and I'll tell every tabloid shark I can

contact about how Maria Santos tried to buy a five-hundred-thousand-dollar commission by seducing a prince." He smiled thinly. "They'll lap it up."

* * * * *

*What will it take for this billionaire prince to realize
he's falling in love with his mistress…?*
Look for
BILLIONAIRE PRINCE, PREGNANT MISTRESS
by Sandra Marton
Available July 2009 from Harlequin Presents®.

We'll be spotlighting a different series every month
throughout 2009 to celebrate our 60th anniversary.

Look for Harlequin® Presents in July!

TWO CROWNS, TWO ISLANDS, ONE LEGACY
A royal family, torn apart by pride and its lust for
power, reunited by purity and passion

Step into the world of Karedes
beginning this July with

BILLIONAIRE PRINCE,
PREGNANT MISTRESS
by
Sandra Marton

Eight volumes to collect and treasure!

THE BELLES OF TEXAS

They're as strong as the state that raised
them. The Belle sisters aren't afraid to go
after what they want, whether it's reclaiming
their ranch or their family.

Linda Warren
CAITLYN'S PRIZE

Thanks to her deceased father's gambling
debts, Caitlyn Belle's beloved High Five Ranch
is in dire straits. Particularly because the
will stipulates that if the ranch doesn't turn
a profit in six months, it must be sold to
Judd Calhoun—the man Caitlyn jilted
fourteen years ago. And Cait knows Judd has
been waiting a long time for his revenge....

*Look for the first book
in The Belles of Texas miniseries,
on sale in July wherever books are sold.*

You're invited to join our Tell Harlequin Reader Panel!

By joining our new reader panel you will:

- Receive Harlequin® books—they are FREE and yours to keep with no obligation to purchase anything!
- Participate in fun online surveys
- Exchange opinions and ideas with women just like you
- Have a say in our new book ideas and help us publish the best in women's fiction

In addition, you will have a chance to win great prizes and receive special gifts!
See Web site for details. Some conditions apply.
Space is limited.

To join, visit us at
www.TellHarlequin.com.

REQUEST YOUR FREE BOOKS!

2 FREE NOVELS PLUS 2 FREE GIFTS!

Silhouette® Desire®

Passionate, Powerful, Provocative!

In 2009 Harlequin celebrates
60 years of pure reading pleasure!

We're marking this occasion by offering
16 **FREE** full books to download and read.

Visit

www.HarlequinCelebrates.com

to choose from a variety of
great romance stories
that are absolutely **FREE!**

(Total approximate retail value of $60)

We invite you to visit and share the Web site
with your friends, family
and anyone who enjoys reading.

COMING NEXT MONTH
Available July 14, 2009

#1951 ROYAL SEDUCER—Michelle Celmer
Man of the Month
The prince thought his bride-to-be knew their marriage was only
a diplomatic arrangement. But their passion in the bedroom tells a
different story….

**#1952 TAMING THE TEXAS TYCOON—
Katherine Garbera**
Texas Cattleman's Club: Maverick County Millionaires
Seducing his secretary wasn't part of the plan—yet now he'll
never be satisfied with just one night.

#1953 INHERITED: ONE CHILD—Day Leclaire
Billionaires and Babies
Forced to marry to keep his niece, this billionaire finds the
perfect solution in his very attractive nanny…until a secret she's
harboring threatens to destroy everything.

#1954 THE ILLEGITIMATE KING—Olivia Gates
The Castaldini Crown
This potential heir will only take the crown on one condition—
he'll take the king's daughter with it!

**#1955 MAGNATE'S MAKE-BELIEVE MISTRESS—
Bronwyn Jameson**
Secretly determined to expose his housekeeper's lies, he makes
her his mistress to keep her close. But little does he know that he
has the wrong sister!

**#1956 HAVING THE BILLIONAIRE'S BABY—
Sandra Hyatt**
After one hot night with his sister's enemy, he's stunned when she
reveals she's carrying his baby!

SDCNMBPA0609